Christmas at
Copper Mountain

Christmas at

Copper Mountain

A TAMING OF THE SHEENANS NOVELLA

JANE PORTER

TULE
PUBLISHING

DEDICATION

For my incredible readers and the wonderful women on the Jane Porter and Montana Born Street Teams. You all make writing a joy. This story is for you!

Chapter One

HARLEY DIEKERHOFF LOOKED up from peeling potatoes to glance out the kitchen window.

It was still snowing… even harder than it had been this morning.

So much white, it dazzled.

Hands still, breath catching, she watched the thick, white flakes blow past the ranch house at a dizzying pace, enthralled by the flurry of the lacy snowflakes.

So beautiful. Magical A mysterious silent ballet in all white, the snow swirling, twirling just like it did in her favorite scene from the Nutcracker—the one with the Snow Queen and her breathtaking corps in their white tutus with their precision and speed—and then that dazzling snow at the end, the delicate flakes powdering the stage.

Harley's chest ached. She gripped the peeler more tightly, and focused on her breathing.

She didn't want to remember.

She wasn't going to remember.

Wasn't going to go there, not now, not today. Not when she had six hungry men to feed in a little over two hours. She picked up a potato, started peeling.

She'd come to Montana to work. She'd taken the temporary job at Copper Mountain Ranch to get some distance from her family this Christmas, and working on the Paradise Valley cattle ranch would give her new memories.

Like the snow piling up outside the window.

She'd never lived in a place that snowed like this. Where she came from in Central California, they didn't have snow, they had fog. Thick soupy Tule fog that blanketed the entire valley, socking in airports, making driving nearly impossible. And on the nights when the fog lifted and temperatures dropped beneath the cold clear sky, the citrus growers rushed to light smudge pots to protect their valuable, vulnerable orange crops.

Her family didn't grow oranges. Her family were Dutch dairy people. Harley had been raised on a big dairy farm in Visalia, and she'd marry a dairyman in college, and they'd had their own dairy, too.

But that's the part she needed to forget.

That's why she'd come to Montana, with its jagged mountains and rugged river valleys and long cold winters.

She'd arrived here the Sunday following Thanksgiving and would work through mid-January, when Brock Sheenan's housekeeper returned from a personal leave of absence.

In January, Harley would either return to California or look for another job in Crawford County. Harley was tempted to stay, as the Bozeman employment agency assured her they'd have no problem finding her a permanent position if she wanted one. So far she liked everything about her job on the isolated ranch, from the icy, biting wind that howled beyond the ranch's thick log cabin walls, to the cooking, cleaning, and laundry required.

The physicality of the work was exactly what her mind and body needed. It was good to lift, bend, carry, mop, sweep, dust, fold. The harder she worked, the better she felt, and today, for the first time in years, she actually felt almost....

Happy.

Harley paused, brows knitting in surprise.

Almost happy.

Wow.

That was huge. Almost happy was significant. Almost happy gave her hope that one day she would feel more again, and be more again, and life wouldn't be so bleak and cold.

Because it had been bleak.

It'd been....

She shook her head, brushed off the little peel clinging to her thumb and grabbed the last potato, swiftly peeling it, clearing her mind of everything but the task at hand, concentrating on the texture of the wet potato, the cool water in the sink, the quick motion of the peeler, the dazzling white flurries at the window, and the crackle of the fire behind her.

She liked being here. It was good being here. This wasn't her house and yet in just one week it felt like home.

She enjoyed this kitchen with its golden, hand-planed pine cabinets, wide-planked hardwood floor, and the corner fireplace rimmed in local rock from the Yellowstone River. She loved how the rustic exterior of the sprawling two-story cabin hid the large, comfortable, efficient kitchen and the adjacent over-sized laundry room with its two sets of washers and dryers... to handle feeding and looking after, not just Brock Sheenan, owner of Copper Mountain Ranch, but the hired hands who worked for Brock and lived in the bunk house behind the barn.

In winter the ranch hands didn't leave the property much during the week. The work was too grueling, the nights fell early, and driving at night could be treacherous on the windy, icy mountain road, so Monday through Friday Brock provided dinners for his five men, and clean, dry clothes, too. Come weekend, they were on their own, but Harley wouldn't have minded cooking for extra mouths seven days a week.

The isolation of Copper Mountain Ranch, tucked back in the Absarokas, higher than the typical Paradise Valley ranch, might have scared off other job applicants, but not her. She didn't mind the severe weather or Brock Sheenan's brusqueness—and she'd been warned about that in advance—but she was okay with a silent, gruff boss. She didn't come to Marietta, Montana looking for friendship. Like Brock himself, she didn't need conversation and company. She was here to work, and she preferred being left alone.

The employment agency liked her attitude. They said she was perfect for the temp job and filled her in on the Sheenans, one of the bigger, more prominent families that had settled in Paradise Valley around the turn of the century. She'd be working for Brock Sheenan, the oldest of the five Sheenan sons. Brock had bought Copper Mountain Ranch to get away from his dad, which had caused some bad blood within the family, but he'd wanted his own place, and had designed the two-story log cabin himself, helping build it as a wedding present for his bride.

But tragedy struck a year and a half into their marriage, when Brock's wife Amy was killed in a horrific car crash on one of the twisting mountain roads. Devastated, Brock disappeared into his ranch, becoming almost reclusive after that.

The employment agency had shared the details with her, asking for her confidence. But they thought it was important she understand that Brock Sheenan had a… reputation… for being eccentric. He didn't need people the way others did, and he'd been quite specific in his desire for a tidy, professional, and disciplined housekeeper. He wouldn't tolerate lazy and he couldn't abide chatty. He needed a quiet, orderly house, and he liked things done his way.

Harley didn't have a problem with that. She was quiet

too, and this year she'd been determined to avoid the holidays, and had deliberately chosen to go away for December, needing to escape her big California family that celebrated Christmas with endless activity, festivities, and fuss.

She loved all her nieces and nephews but this Christmas she didn't want to be around kids. Because this year she wasn't celebrating Christmas. This year there wasn't going to be a tree or trimmings, no stockings, or brightly wrapped toys.

Eyes hot, chest burning, she scooped up the mountain of wet potato scraps, when a deep, rough male voice startled her.

"You okay, Miss Diekerhoff?"

Turning quickly, potato skins still dripping, Harley blinked back tears as she spotted Brock Sheenan standing by the fireplace, warming his hands.

Brock was a big man. He was tall—six one or two—with broad shoulders, a wide muscular chest, and shaggy black hair.

Harley's late husband, David, was Portuguese and darkly handsome, but David was always groomed and polished while the Montana rancher seemed disinclined to comb his hair, or bother with a morning shave.

The truth was, Brock Sheenan looked like a pirate, and never more so than now, with tiny snowflakes clinging to his wild hair and shadowed jaw.

"I'm fine," she said breathlessly, embarrassed. "I didn't hear you come in."

"The faucet was on." He rubbed his hands together, the skin red and raw. "You're not... crying... are you?"

She heard the uncomfortable note in his voice and cringed a little. "No," she said quickly, straightening and squaring her shoulders as she dumped the potato peels into the garbage. "Everything's wonderful."

"So you're not crying?"

"No," she repeated crisply, drying her hands. "Just peeling potatoes for dinner."

Her gaze swept his big frame, seeing the powdered snow still clinging to the hem of his Wrangler jeans that peeked beneath leather chaps and white glitter dusting his black brows. His supple leather chaps weren't for show. It was frigid outside and he'd spent the week in the saddle, driving the last herds of cattle from the back country to the valley below so they could take shelter beneath trees. "Can I get you something?"

"You don't happen to have any coffee left from this morning that you could heat up?"

"I can make a fresh pot," she said, grabbing the glass carafe to fill it with water. "Want regular or decaf?"

He glanced at the clock mounted on the wall above the door and then out the window where the snow flurries were thickening, making it almost impossible to see the tall pine trees marking one corner of the yard. "Leaded," he said.

"Make it strong, too. It's going to be a late night for me."

She added the coffee grounds, and then hit the brew button. "You're heading back out?"

"I'm going to ride back up as soon as I get something warm in me. Thought I'd take some of the breakfast coffee cake with me. If there was anything left."

"There is." She'd already wrapped the remaining slices in foil. He wasn't one to linger over meals, and he didn't like asking for snacks between meals, either. If he wanted something now, it meant he wouldn't be back anytime soon. But it was already after four. It'd be dark within the hour. "It's snowing hard."

"I won't be able to sleep tonight if I don't do a last check. The boys said we've got them all but I keep thinking we're missing one or two of the young ones. Have to be sure before I call it a night."

Harley reached into a cupboard for one of the thermoses she sent with Brock on his early mornings. "What time will you want dinner?"

"Don't know when I'll be back. Could be fairly late, so just leave a plate in the oven for me. No need for you to stay up." He bundled his big arms across his even bigger chest, a lock of thick black hair falling down over his forehead to shadow an equally dark eye.

There was nothing friendly or approachable about Brock when he stood like that. His wild black hair, square jaw, and dark piercing gaze that gave him a slightly threatening air, but Harley knew better. Men, even the most dangerous men, were still mortal. They had goals, dreams, needs. They tried, they failed. They made mistakes. Fatal mistakes.

"Any of the boys going with you?" she asked, trying to sound casual as she wrapped a generous wedge of cheddar cheese in foil, and a hunk of the summer sausage he liked, so he'd have something more substantial than coffee cake for his ride.

He shook his head, then dragged a large calloused hand through the glossy black strands in a half-hearted attempt to comb the tangled strands smooth. "No."

She gave him a swift, troubled look.

He shrugged. "No point in putting the others in harm's way."

Her frown deepened. "What if you get into trouble?"

"I won't."

She arched her brows.

He gave her a quelling look.

She ought to be intimidated by this shaggy beast of a man, but she wasn't. She'd had a husband—a daring, risk-taking husband of her own—and his lapse in judgment had cost them all. Dearly.

"It's dangerous out there," she said quietly. "You shouldn't go alone. They invented the buddy system for a reason."

One of Brock's black eyebrows shot up. "The buddy system."

She ignored the mockery in his dark, deep voice. His voice always surprised her, in part because it was so deep and husky that it vibrated in his chest, making her think of strong, potent drink and shadowy attics and moonlit bedrooms, but also because until now, he'd never said more than a couple of sentences to her.

He wasn't a big talker. But then, he wasn't in the house much. Brock spent most of his time outdoors working, and when he was inside, he sat at his desk, poring over accounting books and papers, or by the fire in the family room reading.

Maybe that's what made her so comfortable here. The silence.

The dearth of conversation. The lack of argument. The absence of tension.

She needed the solitude of the Copper Mountain Ranch. She needed the quiet. The quiet was a balm to her soul. It sounded dreadful put like that. Corny as well as pathetic, but the loss of everything she knew, and everything she was, had changed her. Broken her. All she could do now was continue to mend. Eventually she'd be able to cope with noise and chaos and families again, but not yet. Not for a long, long time.

"I'm sure you've heard of the buddy system," she said flatly. "It's practiced by virtually everyone... including the Boy Scouts."

He gave her another long look, his dark gaze resting on

her as if she were a bit peculiar.

Right now, she felt a bit peculiar.

It would help if he stopped staring at her so hard. His intense scrutiny was making her overly warm, and a little bit dizzy.

"I was never a Boy Scout," he rasped.

Looking at his long shaggy black hair and shadowed jaw, she could believe it. "You're missing the point."

"I get your point." He stalked toward her, his dark gazing holding hers, his jaw hard.

Panicked, she stepped back, and again, as he stepped close, his big body brushing hers as he reached into the cabinet for a mug. "But I'm not a little boy," he added, glancing at her from beneath his thick black lashes, a warning in his dark eyes, "and don't need coddling."

Energy surged through Harley, a hot sharp electric current that made her heart race and her stomach fall. Legs weak, she took another step sideways, increasing the distance between them. "Obviously you're not a child."

He grabbed the pot of coffee, interrupting the brewing cycle to fill his cup. "Then don't treat me like one."

Her heart continued to pound. She wasn't scared but she definitely was... bothered.

Harley bit down on the inside of her cheek, holding back her first angry retort, aware that the kitchen, peaceful until just minutes ago, now crackled with tension.

"You don't think I should worry about you?" she asked,

arms folding across her chest so he couldn't see that her hands were trembling.

"It's not your job to worry about me."

"No, I'm just to worry about your boxers and your stomach," she retorted.

He arched an eyebrow. "Is that appropriate, Miss Diekerhoff?"

His scathing tone made her flush and look away. She bit down on her cheek again, appalled that she was losing her cool now, and counted to ten. She rarely lost her temper but she was mad. Somehow he'd struck a nerve in her... had gotten under her skin.

When she was sure she could speak calmly she managed a terse apology. "I'm sorry. That wasn't appropriate." Then she set the thermos down on the counter—hard, harder than she intended, and the crack of metal against granite sent a loud echo through the kitchen "And you are right. What you do is none of my concern, so go out in the storm, in the dark, all by yourself. As long as I'm getting paid, I won't give it a second thought."

Heart still racing, she fled the kitchen for the adjoining mudroom to move the laundry forward. Tears burned the back of her eyes and she was breathing hard and she didn't even know why she was so upset, only that she was.

She was furious.

Stupid meathead of a man, thinking he was immortal, invincible, that nothing bad could happen...

Swallowing the curses she wouldn't let herself utter aloud, Harley shoved the tangle of heavy, wet jeans and cords from the washer into the dryer.

But testosterone didn't make a man immortal.

Just daring. Risky.

Foolish.

Her chest ached, the pressure on her heart horrendous. If David hadn't been so confident. If David hadn't been such a proud man. If David....

"What's the matter with you?" Brock demanded, filling the laundry room doorway as if it were a sliver of space instead of forty inches wide by eight feet tall. "You're acting like a crazy lady."

Harley jammed the wet clothes into the dryer so hard she slammed her wrist bone on the round barrel opening, sending pain shooting up her arm.

Tears started to her eyes. Worry and regret flooded her. Worry for Brock, and regret that she'd said too much. She wasn't here to talk. She was here to work. She knew that. "I'm not crazy," she retorted huskily, rubbing the tender spot on her wrist. "Don't call me crazy."

"You're behaving in a completely irrational—"

"It's a blizzard outside, Mr. Sheenan. And I was merely asking you to take precautions when you headed back out, and if that makes me crazy, then so be it. I am crazy. Make that a lunatic."

His black eyebrows flattened and he looked at her so

long it crossed her mind that she'd said far too much, pushed too hard, perhaps even lost her job.

And then his dark eyes glimmered and the corner of his mouth lifted faintly. "A lunatic?"

There was something in the way he repeated his words that made her want to smile.

Or maybe it was the shadow in his eyes that looked almost like amusement.

Or that very slight lift of his firm lips.

He seemed to be fighting a smile. Could it be?

If so, it was the closest she'd ever come to seeing him smile. Brock was a serious man. The agency said the death of his wife had changed him.

She understood. It'd been three years since the accident, and she still grieved for David and her children.

Her desire to smile faded. Her heart burned. She opened her mouth to speak but no words came out.

But then, there were no words.

The pain had been unspeakable.

She closed her eyes, held her breath, holding the agony in, and then she found her strength, and exhaled, and met her employer's shuttered gaze.

"Let me fill your thermos," she said unsteadily. "I've got some snacks for your saddlebag, too. Obviously you don't have to take them. It's entirely up to you."

He leaned against the doorframe, blocking her exit. "You're even more bossy than my last housekeeper, and yet you're just half her age. I don't want to know you in twenty years."

And just like that he brought her back to reality. Who they were. Why she was here. His temporary housekeeper.

Harley managed a tight smile. "Good. You won't have to know me in twenty years, because I'm only here until January thirteenth." She looked up at him, expression blank. "And if you don't return tonight, then I suppose I'm free tomorrow." She motioned for him to move, with an impatient gesture of her finger. "Now if you'd please move, I have work to do."

BROCK DIDN'T KNOW if he should throttle his bossy, imperious housekeeper or fire her.

He ought to fire her. Right here, right now. She wasn't the right woman for the job. Wasn't the right woman for him.

He swallowed hard, biting back the sharp retort as he stared down into his housekeeper's startling green eyes.

What the hell was he doing with a beautiful woman for a housekeeper?

Harley Diekerhoff was not supposed to be attractive.

The name wasn't attractive. The name conjured visions of a stout, strong woman with massive forearms and a sprinkling of dark hair above a thin pale lip.

Or so he'd imagined when the temp employment agency had given him her file as the best possible candidate for the six-week position as housekeeper and cook for his ranch.

He'd wanted a stout woman with massive forearms and a hairy upper lip. He'd been confident he'd hired one.

Instead Harley Diekerhoff was beautiful, and young, and probably the best housekeeper he'd ever had.

It pissed him off.

He didn't want a stunning thirty-four-year-old with hauntingly high cheekbones and eyebrows that arched and turned into wings, making him want to look into her cool green eyes again and again.

He didn't want a housekeeper with a wide full-lipped mouth, creamy skin, and thick hair the color of rich, decadent caramel.

And he most certainly didn't want a housekeeper with curves, endless curves, curves that did nothing but tease his control and inflame his imagination.

His jaw tightened. He battled his temper. "Don't get too carried away," he said curtly. "I'll be back tonight. You'll still have a job to do in the morning."

Her tawny eyebrows arched even higher. Her long ponytail slipped over her shoulder. "Good, because I like the job. It's just—" she broke off, lips compressing, swallowing the words.

"What?" he demanded.

She shook her head, white teeth pinching her plump lower lip.

He tried not to focus on the way her teeth squeezed the

soft lip. He didn't want to focus on her at all. "What?" he repeated.

She sighed and glanced down at her hands. "Nothing," she said quietly.

He said nothing.

She sighed again, twisted her hands. "I like it here," she added. "And I like you. So just be careful. That's all."

He stared at her, perplexed.

She was nothing like Maxine, his housekeeper of the past nine years. Maxine didn't laugh or smile or cry. She arrived every morning, did her work, and then left every night when her husband came to pick her up.

Maxine was silent and sober and moved through the house as if invisible.

Harley moved through the house as if a beacon shone on her. She practically glowed, bathed with light.

He didn't understand how she did it, or what she did, only that from the moment she'd arrived seven days ago nothing in this house had been the same.

Suddenly aware that they were standing so close he could smell the scent of her shampoo—something sweet and floral, freesia or orange blossom and entirely foreign in his masculine house—he abruptly stepped back, letting her pass.

His gaze followed her as she crossed the kitchen, hating himself for noticing how the apron around her waist emphasized how small it was as well as the gentle swell of hips. "Just leave my dinner in the oven," he said.

"If that's what you want," she said, reaching for the coffee pot to fill his thermos.

"That's what I want," he growled, looking away, unable to watch her a moment longer because just having her in his house made him feel things he didn't want to feel.

Like desire.

And hunger.

Lust.

He didn't lust. Not anymore. Maybe when he was a kid, young and randy with testosterone, he battled with control, but he didn't battle for control, not at thirty-nine.

At least, he hadn't battled for control in years.

But he was struggling now, inexplicably drawn to this temporary housekeeper who looked so fresh and wholesome in her olive green apron with its sprigs of holly berries that he wanted to touch her. Kiss her. Taste her.

And that was just plain wrong.

He ground his teeth together, held his breath, and cursed the employment agency for sending him a sexy housekeeper.

She walked toward him, held out the filled thermos and foil-wrapped packets of cheese sausage and coffee cake. "Be careful."

He glanced down at her, seeing but not wanting to see how her apron outlined her shape. Hips, full breasts, and a tiny waist he could circle with two hands. Even with her hideous apron strings wrapped twice around her waist.

Aprons were supposed to hide the body. Her apron just

emphasized her curves. And olive was such a drab color but somehow it made her eyes look mysterious and cool and green and her lips dark pink and her skin—

"I'm always careful," he ground out, taking the thermos and foil packages from her, annoyed all over again.

He was a man about to turn forty and he'd spent the past eleven years raising two kids on his own, and he might not be a perfect father or a perfect man but he tried his best. He did. And while he appreciated his new housekeeper's concern, he didn't have time to be babied, and he certainly wasn't about to explain himself. Not to his brothers, his dad, and especially not to a staggeringly pretty woman from California who was now living in his house, under his roof, bending and leaning and doing all sorts of things with her incredibly appealing body, all the while humming as she went about her work as if she were Snow White or Mary Poppins.

Most annoying to have a beautiful housekeeper. He would never have hired her if he'd realized she was so damn pretty. He didn't want pretty in his house. He didn't want to be tempted. He had a ranch to manage and two children who would be home from boarding school for their holidays in another week and he couldn't afford to get distracted by a pretty face or a shapely body.

His gaze narrowed as it swept Harley Diekerhoff's long, lean legs and gently rounded hips before skimming her small waist, then lifting to her face. "Always careful," he repeated, and stalked out through the kitchen door to the back porch.

Harley Diekerhoff might be a perfect cook and house-keeper, but she was also a temptation, and that was a problem he didn't need.

Chapter Two

HARLEY RANG THE bell at six o'clock to let the ranch hands know dinner was ready. Brock had trained his hands to come to the main kitchen to help carry their dinner to the bunkhouse. One by one she handed off the various dishes—the platter of sliced flank steak, a substantial casserole of cheesy potato gratin, two loaves of warm buttered French bread, a bowl of green beans with almonds and bacon, a hefty green salad, and an enormous chocolate sheet cake with a gallon of milk for dessert.

Bundled in her winter coat and mittens, she followed the parade of ranch hands through the swirling snow, careful not to drop the oversized sheet cake with its thick chocolate icing. Brock said the hands didn't need dessert every night. She disagreed. A man always needed something sweet before bed. Made a man feel cared for.

At least that's how she'd been raised.

Young Lewis Dilford, one of the newer hands, held the bunk house's front door open for her. She stomped her fleece-lined all-weather boots on the mat, knocking off snow before stepping into the bunkhouse. A fire burned hotly in the cast iron stove in the corner.

The bunk house was actually the original log cabin on the property, and on her first day at Copper Mountain Ranch, JB, Brock's ranch foreman, gave Harley a tour of the outbuildings, including a walk through the bunk house.

JB told her that when Brock had bought the ranch thirteen years ago his plan had been to tear the old log cabin down and salvage the logs for a future project, but when he discovered that the walls and flooring were still sound, and all the cabin really needed was a new roof and some modernizing, he gutted the one-bedroom cabin, adding electricity and plumbing, a small indoor bathroom, and a working kitchen.

With the exception of some of the electrical work, Brock had done all the remodeling himself. It'd taken him a year to complete the bunk house, but he liked being busy, and it gave him something to do during the summers with the longer days of sunlight.

She glanced around the main room which was both sitting room and dining room. Chairs were pushed back against the wall and the pine dining table was already set.

"It looks nice," she said, complimenting their efforts to make the table look nice with the tablecloth she'd given them.

Her first two nights here they'd ignored the table cloth

she'd brought them. Apparently Maxine didn't care if they used a tablecloth or placemats.

Some of the men weren't sure they needed to use fancy stuff like table cloths, either. But Harley said it just might make dinner a little nicer, and while she couldn't make them use a table cloth, it was their dinner, after all, and they ought to enjoy themselves. Feel good about themselves.

The next night she entered the bunkhouse and found the table covered with the cloth and five place settings of silverware and plates.

She didn't say anything. She didn't have to. They were watching her face and her quick surprised smile told them everything they needed to know. Since then they used the table cloth every night, and lately, they all washed up and combed their hair, too.

The lost boys of Copper Mountain, she thought, smiling a little as she looked at them now.

"I hope you are hungry," she said, placing the cake and the milk on the table next to all the other dishes filling the center of the table. Maxine used to leave all the food on the buffet, but Harley put everything on the table so the men could stay seated and serve themselves family style. "I think I made too much."

Lewis smiled shyly as he took a seat on one of the benches. "Can never have too much, Miss Harley."

She smiled back, aware that he was the youngest in a family of seven, and from what she'd gathered, there hadn't always been enough to eat by the time it was his turn. "Don't worry about bringing the dishes back tonight. Leave them in your sink and I'll get them in the morning."

"That's not the deal, Miss Harley, and you know it," thin, dark bearded Al Mancetti said, boots thudding as he sat down opposite Lewis. He'd been here on the ranch for about five years now and tended to be on the quiet side, but apparently he was one of the hardest workers. "We'll bring everything back. You done enough. And we're grateful. You take care of us real well."

"It's my pleasure," she answered with a smile. She liked these men. She enjoyed taking care of them. They appreciated her and that felt good, too. Normally she left after they had everything but tonight she lingered, mustering the courage to bring up her concerns about their boss. "It's bad outside," she said after a moment.

"Yes, ma'am," JB answered, from his spot at the head of the table. "Biggest storm of the year so far. Four feet in the last couple hours alone."

That wasn't reassuring at all, she thought. "Mr. Sheenan's out there."

"Yes, ma'am," JB agreed.

She glanced out the window at the dark night with the luminous snow reflecting ghostly white beyond the window. "He shouldn't have gone alone."

"He shouldn't have gone at all," JB agreed, "but you don't tell him that."

Her brows knit. "Shouldn't someone go look for him?"

JB grimaced. "He'd have our heads for that, and I like my head where it is, on my shoulders."

A guffaw of masculine laughter sounded around the table, and even Harley smiled faintly before her smile faded. "He could be in trouble," she said hesitantly.

"Sheenan can take of himself," Paul, the youngest hand said. He was close friends with Lewis and when they weren't on the ranch, they competed on the rodeo circuit, traveling together whenever possible. Neither of them made good money on the circuit though, so they needed their jobs here on Copper Mountain Ranch to pay bills. "Nobody would mess with him. At least nobody in his right mind."

Heads nodded and Harley glanced at the faces of the ranch hands.

"What about bears?" she asked.

"What about them?" Paul retorted, leaning across the table to stab his fork into the sliced steak. "It's winter. They're hibernating."

"And wolves?"

"Sheenan has a gun."

Harley's lips pursed, even more alarmed.

Paul and Lewis laughed.

"Don't you worry, Miss Harley," JB said, using the nickname the hands had given her as Miss Diekerhoff was apparently too much of a mouthful, requiring too much effort. "The boss grew up in this part of Montana. He knows what he's doing, and he'll be back before bedtime. Nine or ten and he'll be safe in his bed. Mark my words."

HARLEY RETURNED TO the house and ate her dinner at the oversized island counter that filled the center of the kitchen, the fire warming her back, somewhat soothed by JB's assurance that their boss would be back by nine or ten.

But nine came and went, with no sign of Brock.

And then ten came, and still no sign of him.

Harley dimmed the downstairs lights before heading up to her room, which would be a third floor room if there was a real floor. Instead it was a room carved out from beneath the massive wood beams of the steeply sloping roof. The walls were all lined with planks of weathered, recycled wood—boards taken from old Montana barns—and her bed sat between two low antique chests with matching antique brass lamps. The bed linens were a neutral taupe on cream stripe, which added the rustic feel. The only real color was the deep crimson wool carpet on the hardwood floor. The pop of red made Harley smile, but tonight as she climbed into bed, she didn't feel much like smiling.

It was hard to relax and fall asleep with knots in her stomach. She knew too well that accidents happened, and even smart, strong people could be overly confident of their skills. How could she sleep, picturing Brock lying buried in the snow, slowly freezing to death?

As her bedside clock showed eleven, Harley wondered if

she should call the police, or maybe someone in Brock's family.

His father wasn't that far, another ranch twenty minutes south in Paradise Valley, and he had four brothers, although none lived in the area at the moment. But surely one of them would want to know that Brock was missing.

Surely something should be done.

She left bed to pace her room, a long black oversized cashmere sweater around her shoulders for warmth, with the antique wool carpet soft beneath her bare feet.

She was still pacing when she heard an engine outside. A truck was approaching the house. As she headed for the window, bright headlight beams pierced the crack in her curtains, sending an arc of white light across her dark bedroom.

Someone was here.

She pushed aside the curtain, and peered down. A big four-by-four truck with snow tires pulled into the circular drive in front of the house. The truck parked, headlights turned off.

She watched as the driver's door opened, and then the passenger door, too. A man with fair hair wearing a heavy sheepskin coat stepped down from the driver's side of the truck and two children climbed more slowly from the passenger side. All three tramped through the thick snow that had piled up since she shoveled the walkway late in the afternoon.

It was after eleven at night. Who would be arriving now? And with kids?

Harley was at the top of the second floor landing when the doorbell rang.

Downstairs, she opened the door, and blinked at the bite of cold wind. It'd stopped snowing hours ago but tiny flakes swirled and trembled around them as the frigid gust of air sent the powdery snow tumbling from the trees to the ground.

"Can I help you?" she asked, pulling her sweater closer to her body as she glanced from the blond man to the two children at his side. The children, dressed in school uniforms, looked half-frozen without proper winter coats, their navy wool blazers with the red and gold school insignia on the chest, inadequate for the low Montana temperature.

"I'm Sheriff O'Dell," the man said, introducing himself, before pointing to the kids. "These two look familiar?"

Harley glanced down at the two pre-adolescents, the boy with dark hair, the girl's a light reddish brown. Both of their pale faces were lightly freckled. "No," she said, confused. "Should they?"

The sheriff frowned. "They say they belong here."

The girl rolled her eyes. "We *live* here." She pushed past Harley to enter the house, her back pack knocking the door wide open. "Where's Dad?"

"Dad?" Harley repeated, hugging the wall, watching the boy follow the girl in.

"Yes, Dad," the girl replied, glaring at Harley. "Brock Sheenan. Heard of him?"

Harley blinked, taken aback. "Uh, yes. Of course. I'm his housekeeper—"

"Where's Maxine?" the girl interrupted. "Don't tell me Dad got rid of Maxine?"

"No," Harley answered, bundling her arms across her chest, shocked, chilled, unable to process that Brock had kids. He'd never once mentioned kids to her. "She took a personal leave but will be back in January."

"Good." The girl's narrowed gaze swept Harley. " 'Cause for a minute there I thought Dad had a girlfriend."

Harley stared at the girl, absolutely blindsided. "And you are...?"

"Molly," the girl said promptly. "And that's Mack."

"We're twins," Mack said, giving Harley a shy smile as he set his back pack down in the hall. "Don't mind Molly. She was just born this way."

"Shut up, Lady Gaga," Molly retorted, punching the boy's shoulder, but it wasn't very hard. "And I got us home. You didn't think I could."

"Well, actually Sheriff O'Dell got us home—"

"From Marietta. But I got us to Marietta from New York," she flashed, nose lifting. "And that was the hard part."

"Just glad we're here." Mack glanced around. "Where is Dad? Is he here?"

"No," Harley said shivering. She honestly didn't know

what to make of any of this. "He should be back anytime though. I'd actually expected him before now." She gestured for the sheriff to enter the house so she could close the door.

"Is he out of town?" The sheriff asked, taking off his hat as he entered the house.

"No. He's... out on the property." Harley grimaced. "On horseback."

The sheriff frowned but the kids didn't look perturbed. Mack actually nodded. "He's probably looking for a cow," he said.

Harley glanced at the boy. "Yes."

"That's Dad. He can't sleep if he thinks one of them might be in trouble."

The sheriff looked from the kids to Harley. "So I can leave them here with you? I've got a little girl of my own at home with a sitter, and I ought to get back... if you're okay here."

Harley looked at the pale, wan faces of Brock's twins. They were obviously exhausted. And cold. "Yes," she said, wondering just what the story was here. Surely Brock should have mentioned that he had kids arriving tonight...

Surely he should have mentioned he had kids...

Surely at some point in the hiring process *someone* should have mentioned that he had kids...

The Sheriff reached into his pocket and gave her his card. "If there's a problem, you've got my number, and the office number. Call me."

Harley thanked him for his time and assistance, and then he was off and the front door closed again behind him, leaving her alone with the two kids in the hall.

For a moment they all just stood there and then Harley drew a deep breath, not at all sure what to say, but something needed to be said. "This is a surprise. Your... dad... didn't mention you were coming."

The twins exchanged glances. For a moment there was just silence. Then Mack spoke. "Dad didn't know we were coming... now. He's uh... going to be... surprised."

Brock was going to be surprised?

Things were getting even more interesting. "So he didn't expect you?" Harley asked.

Mack shook his head.

"Why not?"

The kids glanced at each other again. Molly made a face. "School doesn't get out for the Christmas for another week."

"Ten days, actually," Mack muttered.

Harley's eyebrows lifted. "And you go to school where?"

"New York." Mack looked up at her from beneath his lashes. He had a mop of thick, dark hair and his dark brown eyes were exactly the same shade as his father's. Definitely Brock's boy. "It's a boarding school."

"Which we *hate*," Molly said fiercely, shortly, shivering. She had dark shadows beneath her blue-gray eyes that made her freckles stand out even more. "So we're home."

Harley gazed down at the children, thinking they

couldn't be much older than ten or eleven. "And you got to Marietta from New York on your own?"

They nodded in unison.

"We took a train and then a bus." Molly sounded proud, even though she was still shivering. "But now we're broke."

Harley still had a dozen more questions but realized they weren't important now. The kids were freezing and had to be hungry and tired. "Grab your back packs. Show me your rooms," she said, unable to imagine the kids in the two guest rooms on the second floor, rooms she kept clean and pristine with daily dusting but it was impossible to picture the kids in those rooms. They were handsome enough rooms, but totally impersonal.

Upstairs, Harley's heart fell as Mack opened the first door on the right. "My room," he said, swinging his back pack onto the full size bed with rustic headboard. The walls were recycled barn planks, just like her room and a red, taupe, and green Native American blanket covered the duvet. A framed antique flag hung on the wall and some old iron brands hung on another wall and those were the only decorative elements.

Harley had been in this room daily and it had never once crossed her mind that it belonged to a child. Where were the toys and posters and framed pictures? Where were the bright colors and fun pillows and stuffed animals?

"This looks so adult," she said, trying to sound complimentary, even as she remembered the murals she'd painted in her own children's rooms, and the colorful matching duvet covers and shams she'd sewn to match the murals. Each of her three had picked out his or her own theme: Ariel and Under the Sea, Peter Pan and Never-Never Land, The Cheshire Cat from Alice and Wonderland.

Molly smothered a yawn. "Dad doesn't do baby-stuff." She gestured toward the door. "Let me show you my room."

Mack followed them down the hall, and the three entered the second bedroom.

Molly switched on the light. "This is my room," she said. Her back pack fell to the floor with a dull thud.

Harley could see it was a slightly more feminine room. The headboard was an old European piece from the 1800s. Harley imagined the tall, austere headboard had come over with a German or Scandinavian immigrant family. The linens were pale and a deep red velvet tapestry blanket was folded across the foot of the bed. An antique oval mirror hung on one wall. A small framed quilt hung on another wall.

"Very pretty," Harley said, heart falling a little more, because the rooms were comfortable and the furniture was solid and the linens were attractive. But the bedrooms lacked life and warmth. They needed photos and knick knacks and posters to make the space personal. The twins were pre-teens. Shouldn't their bedrooms reflect their style?

She turned to look at the kids. They were drooping with cold and exhaustion. She hadn't planned on children being here, but now that they were here, she couldn't ignore them. Not when they looked so pitiful. She drew a quick breath, mustered a smile. "Why don't you two shower and change and get warm, and I'll go make you something to eat?"

Mack nodded eagerly. "Yes, please. I'm *starving*."

"Haven't had dinner," Molly said.

"Or lunch," Mack added.

The kids exchanged quick glances.

"Or much of anything since we left the school yesterday," Molly said wrinkling her nose.

Harley felt her insides tighten, churn. These kids had been through a lot and it troubled her but right now the most important thing was getting them warm and fed. "Grilled cheese sound all right?" she asked.

Both kids nodded.

"Good. I'll bring dinner trays up to your rooms, okay?"

"Okay," Molly said.

Mack shook his head. "We can't." He looked at Molly, and shook his head again. "You know we can't eat in our rooms. It's one of Dad's rules." He glanced to Harley, his expression apologetic. "We're only allowed to eat at the dining room table."

"Not in the kitchen at the counter?' Harley asked, trying to figure out the rules, because there seemed to be quite a few of them.

"No." Mack shrugged. "But it's okay. Some people never eat at the dining room table together. We're lucky we do."

For a moment Harley didn't know if she should laugh or cry. Her lips eventually curved into a reluctant smile. "You're right. I'll see you downstairs."

IT WAS CLOSE to one when Harley heard heavy footsteps on the back porch. She'd curled up in the rocking chair next to the kitchen fire and had dozed while waiting for Brock's return.

The stomp of his feet outside the kitchen door woke her. She was on her feet in a flash, opening the door to greet him.

"You're back," she said low, indignantly. She couldn't help it. It's been a long, worrying night. And it was all his fault.

He knocked the snow off his hat and looked at her where she stood in the doorway. "Yes." His lips curved grimly. "Disappointed?"

She wrapped her arms around her to stay warm, her breath clouding in little white puffs. "No. Relieved." She drew her arms even more tightly across her chest. "You have kids." The words tumbled from her. "Two. A boy and a girl."

His eyes narrowed. He frowned, creases in his broad brow. "Yes."

"They're eleven."

His frown deepened. "They're twins."

"Mack and Molly."

His black brows flattened as he shrugged off his snow

35

crusted coat and hung it up on the peg outside the kitchen door. "And this is important… why?"

Her jaw tightened. Of course he'd say that. Tonight as she'd sat in the rocking chair she'd thought about everything that had happened today and it struck her that Brock wasn't reserved. He was rude. "It's important because they're *here*."

His dark gaze shot past her to the dimly lit house. "Here?"

"Yes, Mr. Sheenan. They arrived this evening around eleven, while you were out."

"At the house?"

"Yes. They're upstairs sleeping now. I fed them dinner and put them to bed."

"Huh," he grunted, stepping around her to enter the house. Make that, *push* his way into the house.

Just as Molly had when she'd arrived.

Harley bit her lip, thinking that Mack might have inherited his dad's dark good looks, but Molly had his personality and temper. She followed him into the kitchen where he dropped his damp felt hat on the counter and tugged off his leather work gloves. Melting snow dripped from the hem of his chaps.

His gaze was fixed on the hall with the view of the staircase. "Sleeping, you said?"

She battled her temper, closing the kitchen door and locking it with the dead bolt. "I hope they're sleeping. It's almost one in the morning."

He said nothing to this, crossing to the fireplace to sit down in the rocking chair she'd just vacated. He worked one wet boot off, and then another. The kitchen's lights were turned low and the kitchen was shadowy, save for the red glow of the fire which still burned with a good-sized log. "You kept the fire burning," he said.

"You weren't home," she answered, standing next to the counter, watching him, thinking that everything had changed. Her feelings about being here had changed. She didn't want to be here anymore.

For a moment there was just silence and she curled her fingers into the edge of her fuzzy sleeve, making fists out of her curled fingers.

She should just go to bed right now, before anything else was said.

She should just go to bed before she said something she'd regret.

But she couldn't make herself walk out. Couldn't leave. She was still too upset. Too shocked. Too worried.

Brock Sheenan was a widower, with kids, and his kids were good kids but they were lonely and homesick and being raised with a lot of tough love. Harley came from a strict Dutch family. She understood rules and order but she'd also been raised with plenty of affection, and laughter, and fun.

After sitting with Mack and Molly while they wolfed down their grilled cheese sandwiches and tomato soup, Harley wasn't sure the twins had known a lot of hugs and kisses and laughter.

And that ate at her.

It ate at her after they'd gone to sleep. It ate at her as she sat in the rocking chair. It ate at her now.

Brock leaned back in the rocking chair, his big shoulders filling the entire space, his chest so broad it made the oversized rocking chair look small. "Spit it out," he said.

Harley's fists squeezed tighter. "Spit it out?"

His dark head inclined. "You're obviously dying to say something. So say it. I'm tired. Hungry. I want to eat and go to bed."

She drew a breath and fought for calm. She had to be calm. Men didn't like hysterical women. "You didn't mention them, Mr. Sheenan."

The rocking chair tipped back. He looked at her from under very dark lashes, his dark gaze almost black in the shadowy kitchen. "I didn't know they were coming."

"But you never mentioned them."

"So?"

"So? I'd think you'd mention it when applying for a housekeeper. The agency never mentioned kids. You never mentioned kids. But you have kids, two of them, and they're here for the holidays."

His brow lowered. "They shouldn't be here yet." He paused, thought. "What is the date?"

"December 8th. It's a Sunday."

He said nothing.

She swallowed her impatience. "I arrived a week ago to-day, on the first. I've been here a week."

Frowning, he gazed at the fire. "They weren't supposed to be here until the nineteenth. That's when school gets out for the holidays," he added, half under his breath.

"Does it not... worry... you that they're here?" she asked. She waited for him to say something. He seemed in no hurry to speak, so she pressed on. "Does it not trouble you that two eleven-year-olds, who go to school in *New York*, are on your doorstep in *Montana* at eleven at night?"

"It most definitely concerns me," he said finally, looking at her. He rubbed a hand slowly across his bristled jaw. "But you said they were asleep. What do you want me do? Go haul them out of bed and interrogate them in the middle of the night?"

Her eyes burned and she looked away, staring into the glowing embers of the fire. She couldn't do this. Couldn't be part of this. She didn't want children or Christmas or a pirate for a boss.

"No, of course not," she said, her voice dropping, deepening. "I just... don't understand. How you could not know the kids were missing from school. Shouldn't the school have called you? Shouldn't you have been on a plane the moment you heard that no one could find your twins?"

He closed his eyes, grimaced. "The school probably did call. I'm sure if I checked my phone there would be messages. But I rarely keep it on me as it doesn't work in the back country so no, I don't pay much attention to it."

Or your kids, she wanted to add.

She didn't.

Her fingers twisted, tugging on the fuzzy sweater sleeve. "But why would you never mention them to me? Why would you never once mention that those two guest rooms were actually your children's rooms and you expected your kids home on the nineteenth for their school holiday?"

He shrugged. "I didn't think it mattered."

She bundled her arms across her chest, cold, so cold. "How could they not matter?"

He leaned forward, his dark gaze skewering her. "I did not say *they* didn't matter. I said I didn't think it mattered if *you* knew." His jaw hardened and a small muscle popped in his square jaw, near his ear. "And don't do that again. Put words in my mouth. I may not be president of the PTA, but I love my kids."

"Then why don't you have any pictures of them? Why don't you have any of their artwork framed? Where are their books and toys—"

"I don't like clutter."

"What about them? What about what they like?"

"Pardon me?" He was on his feet, towering over her.

Her heart raced, blood roaring in her ears. He didn't just look like a savage with the fire's flickering flames casting a glow over his hard features, he sounded like a savage, too. But she wasn't intimidated. She'd been through far too much in life to be intimidated by an eccentric mountain man. "You never once mentioned them to me in a week of working here. I had no idea that those two bedrooms I was dusting every day were your children's rooms. I had no idea that two eleven-year-olds would be showing up here on the nineteenth for their Christmas holidays."

"Clearly their arrival has upset you."

Harley's lips tightened. Her heart thudded uncomfortably hard. "No. They haven't upset me. You have upset me."

"Me?"

"Yes, *you*. You are painfully out of touch as a father, more worried about a young cow than your eleven-year-olds, who arrived in Marietta after an all-night Greyhound bus ride after a train ride, as well a lift from a local sheriff who found them at the bus station in downtown Marietta. He thought they were runaways, and then they told him they were yours."

"Your point?"

"You should have known they'd left the school. You should have known they were missing and you should have been out there looking for them the way you were searching for that damn cow." Her chin jerked up, her eyes stinging as she fought emotion she didn't want to feel. "I don't know why they came home early, only that they did, and they were desperate and determined to come home." She blinked hard, trying to clear her eyes before tears welled. "And you should have been here, to greet them. You should have been the one at the door. Not another housekeeper."

His gaze narrowed. He studied her for a long moment, dark lashes lowered over penetrating eyes. "Quite the expert, aren't you?"

His scathing tone wounded. She winced, but wasn't surprised he was angry. He was a man, a thirty-nine year old man, and of course he wouldn't like being criticized.

"I don't belong here," she said, by way of an answer. It wouldn't serve to get into an argument. She'd leave, find another position. It was the only way. She couldn't be here, with the kids, not like this. It'd tear her apart. Break her heart which was only starting to heal. "I'll call the agency in the morning—"

"You dislike kids that much?" he interrupted harshly.

She flinched. "I don't dislike kids."

"Then why leave? You told me just this afternoon you liked it here, you were happy here."

"That was before."

"Before what?"

"Before I knew about…" Her voice faded, she swallowed hard. "The twins."

"If you'd known about them… what? You wouldn't have taken the job here?"

She hesitated, knowing that the truth would damn her.

But the job was no longer the same position she'd accepted. She'd thought she'd left California and her family and their big Christmas to spend the holidays in the middle of nowhere Montana with a dour rancher and five surly ranch hands. That was the job she'd accepted, and wanted.

And she had loved being here this past week. She loved the granite face of the mountain, the towering pine trees, the pastures tucked into the valleys, as well as the silence and freedom from everything she knew in Central California.

Harley drew a deep breath, aware that she hadn't yet answered Brock Sheenan's question. "Probably not," she whispered.

"*Seriously?*"

The harsh, incredulous note in his voice put a lump in her throat. She bit her tongue to keep from saying more. She'd already said too much.

"You hate kids that much?" he demanded.

She looked away, pain rippling through her even as tension crackled in the kitchen. He didn't understand and she wasn't sure she could make him understand, not tonight. Not when she was so tired and barely keeping it together. But the austerity of life here on frigid Copper Mountain Ranch with its gusts of icy wind and blizzard-like storms had been good for her. It allowed her to work and not feel.

It was good not to feel.

It was even better not to want, or need.

"Miss Diekerhoff?"

She turned her head, looked at him. "I don't hate them at all," she said lowly. "I like children very much."

"Then what are you saying?"

She stared at him, stomach churning, heart thudding, aching. "I'm saying that I don't belong here, and that I didn't understand the situation here—" she broke off, gulping air for courage, before pressing on, "—but now that I do, it's better if I leave."

"*What?*"

"I'm sorry."

"I'm shocked. I can't believe this. I can't believe *you*."

Harley couldn't hold his gaze any longer. The censure was too much. "I'll call the agency first thing in the morning and they should be able to send out a temporary replacement that should get you through the weekend—"

He laughed, a dark low bitter laugh that silenced her. "I see. I'll get a temp for my temp? That's great. That's wonderful. Thank you, Miss Diekerhoff, for a fantastic week but maybe I shouldn't be surprised you're walking out on us. Deep down I knew you were too good to be true."

Chapter Three

I KNEW YOU were too good to be true.

The words echoed in Harley's head all night, making her heart hurt and sleep impossible. How could she sleep when every time she closed her eyes, she saw the censure in his dark eyes? Heard the disappointment in his deep voice?

She didn't like disappointing people. And she really didn't like disappointing him.

It's not as if she needed Brock's good opinion. When she left here, she'd never see him again, never have any contact. It shouldn't matter what he thought, or how he said things...

But it did.

She didn't know why. She didn't understand it, but there was something about him that resonated with her. She identified with his silence and rough edges, as well as the deep grief that had made him retreat from the world.

She'd wanted to die after the plane crash that took her family, but her parents and brothers and sisters wouldn't let her quit.

They urged her to cling to her faith.

They told her she still had them.

They reminded her that she was still young with a whole future ahead of her.

She'd weathered the worst of the grief and now she was trying to move forward, putting one foot in front of the other, but it didn't mean she was whole and strong yet.

She still found certain things heartbreakingly painful. Like holidays. And children.

Put the two together and it made her sick with grief.

She wanted her children back. Wanted Emma, Ana, and Davi, nestled close, sitting pressed to her side as they used to when they'd watch a favorite holiday program like Rudolph the Red-Nosed Reindeer or The Grinch that Stole Christmas.

Her kids had loved Christmas and she'd loved giving them the most magical Christmas possible…

Her eyes burned and pain splintered inside her heart, making her want to cry aloud.

She pressed her fists to her eyes to keep the tears from falling. She wouldn't cry. She wouldn't. Tears changed nothing and she had to keep it together. Keep it together and move on.

One step at a time.

One day at a time.

She'd get there. She would.

HARLEY WOKE EARLY despite not falling to sleep until after three. Downstairs in the kitchen she made coffee and a cinnamon bread her kids had loved called Monkey Bread, hoping the warm gooey cinnamon bread would be a peace offering.

It wasn't.

Brock didn't speak to her when he came downstairs at six. He filled his coffee cup and stalked out.

Her sticky sweet pull-apart cinnamon bread went uneaten.

Late morning Harley stood on the front porch of the ranch house, cell phone pressed to her ear, as she spoke with the manager of the Marietta employment agency for the third time in the past two hours.

The manager had finally found someone to replace Harley, but the new temp couldn't start until Saturday.

"Saturday?" Harley cried, listening to the manager even as she kept an eye on the barn door, as the twins had disappeared inside, swaddled in puffy winter coats, scarves, hats and boots. "That's six days from now."

"Five, if you don't count today," the manager answered.

Harley was most certainly counting today "You can't get anyone sooner?"

"It took us weeks to find you, Miss Diekerhoff. You don't just pull good temps out of a hat."

Harley suppressed a sigh, acknowledging that was probably true. And she wouldn't want the agency to send just anyone here to the ranch. You couldn't put just anyone in a house with two pre-teens. The agency would have to do thorough criminal background checks.

Speaking of two pre-teens, Harley glanced at the barn again, wondering what the twins were doing.

The kids hadn't spoken to her this morning, avoiding her since Brock had woken up and talked to them in their rooms. Then all three came downstairs and he'd made eggs and bacon for the kids, and sat with them in the dining room, but there hadn't been much conversation at breakfast, and when Brock did speak to his kids, his tone was quite severe. He was clearly upset with them.

When the twins finished their tense breakfast, they'd carried their dishes in, washed them at the sink and then quietly slipped out, avoiding her.

Upstairs, twenty minutes later, Harley discovered the twins had made their beds and already disappeared outside. Again avoiding her.

She knew then that Brock had said something to the twins, telling them to stay out of her way. She ought to be glad she didn't have them underfoot, but their distance and silence made her unaccountably sad.

Harley forced her attention to the phone call. "So Saturday for sure," she said.

"Yes. We have someone finishing a job elsewhere Friday, so Saturday she'll start at Copper Mountain Ranch."

"Okay," Harley said quietly.

"Can you survive that long?"

Harley ignored the sarcasm in the manager's voice. "Things are pretty... tense... here."

"I'm sure they are. Mr. Sheenan is very unhappy, as we are, too. You've put us all in quite a bind, and we've lost a great deal of credibility with Mr. Sheenan."

"I understand," she said, spotting Mack and Molly who'd just emerged from the barn with an old sled and were dragging it off toward a break in the pine trees. There must be a sledding hill somewhere back behind the trees.

"If we should find someone sooner, I will of course let you know."

"Thank you." Harley drew a quick breath. "And will you be able to find me another job in Marietta, or...?"

"No. I don't think so. Forgive me for being blunt, but we've lost face, and I don't think we can recommend you with confidence to any of our clients or accounts here. Now, if you could turn the situation around and find a way to make the job work, then maybe we will all feel differently."

BACK INSIDE THE house, Harley took off her coat, hanging it up on a peg in the laundry room and then went to the kitchen to figure out what she'd make for dinner.

For long moments she stared blindly into the refrigerator, trying to come up with a plan, but she couldn't focus on anything, too much in a daze.

Everything had gotten so messed up, so fast.

"I thought you'd be packing," Brock said shortly, entering the kitchen to refill his coffee cup.

Harley straightened, shut the refrigerator door, and faced him. "The agency can't replace me until Saturday." She drew a quick breath, tried to smile, but failed. "Looks like you're stuck with me until the weekend."

"You must be devastated," he said, his expression hard.

His sarcasm stung. She struggled to keep her composure.

"Trapped here with children," he added bitingly.

This time she couldn't hide the hurt, her lips trembling, her eyes gritty and hot. "You're making this something it's not," she whispered. "I don't hate kids. I don't dislike them."

His fierce dark gaze met hers and held. "But the moment you found out I had kids you wanted to bolt. True?"

Her lips parted but no sound came out. How to tell him that she'd loved her children so much that when they died it'd killed her?

How to explain that even now, three years without her children, she still woke up in a cold sweat missing them? Needing them?

She gave her head the smallest of shakes. "It's not what you think." Her voice was all but inaudible. "It's a... a... personal... thing."

"Obviously."

She struggled to add. "It's more of a... grief... thing."

He grew still. His dense black lashes lifted. He stared at her hard, searchingly. "You don't have kids."

"No."

His gaze continued to hold hers. "You wanted them?"

She reached for a damp dishtowel by the sink. "Yes."

He said nothing, just looked at her. But it was enough.

Terrified she'd cry or fall apart, she forced herself to action, swiping the dishtowel across the counter, mopping up the glisten of water on the counter. She dragged the dishtowel over another area, this one clean and dry, but activity was good. Activity would distract both of them. Or so she prayed.

But the silence in the kitchen was intolerable. It seemed to stretch on forever.

Finally he spoke. "So you're here for the rest of the week."

"Yes."

"You can handle that?"

"Yes," she said lowly.

"You're sure?"

"*Yes.*"

He turned to leave but stopped in the doorway. "Not that it makes a difference, but they won't require much from you. Just meals, laundry, that sort of thing. I'll keep them out of your way. That should help."

She couldn't look at him. She turned away, feeling naked, and bereft. Harley didn't even know this family and yet she liked them... cared for them. How could she not?

Two freckle-faced eleven-year-olds who'd grown up without a mom.

A darkly handsome rancher who'd become Marietta's

recluse.

This big, handsome log cabin house that lacked the tenderness that would make it a home.

"You don't have to tell them to stay out of my way," she said hoarsely, keeping her face averted. "They're fine. It'll be fine. I promise."

BROCK NODDED SHORTLY and walked out, allowing the kitchen door to slam behind him, glad to escape the kitchen and the grief he'd seen in Harley's face before she'd turned away from him.

He wished he hadn't seen it. He didn't like it, uncomfortable with sorrow and emotions, and already overwhelmed by the twins' sudden arrival home.

The twins weren't supposed to be here, and he was furious with the school and his kids and Harley Diekerhoff for stating the obvious last night—he was not paying his kids enough attention.

But his kids wanted the wrong kind of attention and he wasn't about to reward them for bad behavior.

He grabbed his heavy coat from the hook outside the door, and his dogs came bounding through the snow, the Australian shepherds having deserted him earlier to trail after the kids.

The kids.

Brock's jaw jutted, furious and frustrated. His kids were in so much trouble. Not only had they cut out of school a week early before the school holiday had officially begun, they'd taken two different Amtrak trains and a Greyhound bus to get back to Marietta.

He couldn't even fathom the risks they'd taken, getting home.

He'd taught them to be smart and self-reliant so he wasn't surprised that they could find their way home from New York—after all, they'd all traveled together to the school by train last August, taking the train from Malta to Chicago and then connecting to the Lake Shore Limited, with its daily service between Chicago and New York—but running away from school wasn't smart, or self-reliant. It was stupid. Foolish. Dangerous.

Heading toward the barn, dogs at his heels, Brock shied away from thinking about all the different things that could have gone wrong. There were bad people in this world, people Mack and Molly had never been exposed to, and for all the twins' confidence, they were hopelessly naïve.

Pushing open the barn door, Brock heard the scrape of shovel and rake. Good. The twins were working. He'd told them they couldn't play until they'd mucked out the stalls, a job that would take a couple of hours, and when he'd checked on them twenty minutes ago, he'd discovered they'd cut out to go sledding.

Now they had to muck the stalls and clean and oil the leather bridles… and there were a lot of bridles.

Mack glanced up glumly as Brock came around the corner.

Molly didn't even look at her dad.

"Looks good," Brock said, inspecting the completed stalls. "Just the bridles and you'll be free for the day."

"We really have to take all the bridles, all apart?" Mack asked, groaning. "We just can't wipe them down with leather cleaner?"

"We already talked about this," Brock answered. "I want every buckle undone, all leather pieces shiny with oil and then rubbed down so you get the old wax and dirt off. With a clean cloth, polish the leather up, use an old toothbrush on the bit, cleaning that too, and then put it back together... the right way. If you have to draw a sketch, or take a picture to help you remember how each bridle goes together, then do it, because the job's not finished until the bridles are back hanging in the tack room."

Molly glared at him. "That's going to take all day."

"You're not on vacation, Molly. You were supposed to be in school."

"I *hate* the Academy."

"Then you should enjoy helping out around here. You'll be working all week."

HARLEY DIDN'T SEE the kids again until just an hour before dinner. It was dark outside when they opened the back door to troop dispiritedly through the kitchen. They'd forgotten to take their boots off and they left icy, mucky footprints across the hardwood floor before disappearing upstairs.

Harley paused from mashing the potatoes to run a mop across the floor. She was just finishing by the back door when it opened again and Brock stood there.

"Careful," she said. "It's wet. You don't want to slip."

"Why are you mopping now?" he asked, easing off his boots and leaving them outside.

"It'd gotten dirty and I didn't want everyone walking through it, tracking mud through the rest of the house."

He stepped inside and closed the door behind him. "The kids?"

"It's fine."

"It's not fine. They know to take their boots off. That's one of Maxine's big rules. She'd throw them out if they tramped mud and snow through the house." He walked into the laundry, flipping on the light. "Where are their dirty clothes?"

Harley straightened. "I don't know."

"They haven't brought them down yet?"

"I haven't seen them, no."

"They're testing you, Miss Diekerhoff. They know the rules."

"I don't know the rules, Mr. Sheenan."

"Then maybe you need to ask."

Harley lifted her chin, refusing to be cowed. "What are the house rules, Mr. Sheenan?"

"I'll send the twins down. They'll fill you in."

Chapter Four

HARLEY WENT TO bed Monday night, exhausted and frazzled.

She'd gone from relishing each day at Copper Mountain Ranch to counting down the days until she could leave. The twins didn't like her much. And Brock Sheenan seemed to like her even less.

It was one thing to feed and clothe people. It was another thing to feed and clothe unhappy people. And the twins were certainly unhappy.

Fortunately, Tuesday passed without incident. Brock gave the twins chores, and the kids did their chores, and stayed out of her way.

Tuesday night Brock and his hands didn't come in for dinner as limbs on a massive tree, weighted by snow and ice, snapped, taking down a long section of fence, allowing cattle to wander.

While Brock and the hands repaired the fence and tracked down the missing cattle, Harley fed the twins dinner, serving them at the kitchen counter.

"We're not supposed to eat here," Mack reminded her. "Dad's rules."

Harley filled their glasses with milk. "I asked your dad about that. He said it was Maxine's rule, not his, and since Maxine isn't here, I'm feeding you where I want to feed you."

The twins looked at each other.

"Dad might get mad," Mack added.

Harley placed the milks in front of the kids. "I'm not afraid of your dad, or Maxine. And besides, its nicer eating in here. It's warm and cheerful. The dining room depresses me."

The kids looked at each other again.

"Why does it depress you?" Molly asked, intrigued.

"It's not very cozy."

"Dad doesn't do cozy," Molly said. "Or holidays, or anything festive." She sighed, and stabbed her fork in her chicken. "He used to like Christmas. But not anymore."

Harley turned down the oven to make sure she didn't dry the chicken out. "What do you do for Christmas? How do you celebrate? I noticed you don't have any Advent Calendars out."

"What are Advent Calendars?" Mack asked.

Harley drew a stool out and sat down. "They're a calendar to help you count down to Christmas. Some of them have chocolates, others have little toys. They're just fun."

"Oh, then we definitely wouldn't have them," Molly said. She took a bite and chewed for a long time. After she swallowed, she shrugged. "We don't even decorate anymore."

Harley couldn't believe this. "Nothing?"

"Nope."

"What about a tree?"

"Nope."

"Not even a wreath or garland or candles?"

Molly shook her head. "Dad stopped a couple of years ago with all that stuff. He said it was a waste of time, and expensive."

Harley struggled to hide her horror. "What about presents? Stockings?"

"We get a few presents, mostly practical stuff. But we didn't have stockings last year. Dad said we're too old. Santa doesn't exist." Mack made a face. "And I know Santa isn't real. We figured that out a long time ago, but he didn't have to say it like that. It kind of made us feel bad."

Harley could believe it. Just listening to the twins talk made her feel bad. "Well, maybe we could do something fun while I'm here."

The twins looked skeptical. "Like what?" Molly asked.

"Bake cookies or make a gingerbread house."

Mack frowned. "I've never made a gingerbread house."

"I don't know that I'd want to make a gingerbread house," Molly retorted.

Harley shrugged and rose from the stool. "You're right. Why frost cookies or decorate a gingerbread house and drink hot spiced apple cider, when you can shovel manure and stack hay bales?"

WEDNESDAY MORNING AFTER starting the laundry and tidying all the bathrooms and giving the hardwood floor a good sweep, Harley put on her snow boots and heavy jacket and gloves and headed outside to cut some fragrant pine boughs.

JB, who was on the smaller snowplow, clearing the path between the house and barn, and barn and bunk house, turned off the engine to ask Harley if she needed help.

"I think I've got it," Harley said, shaking the armful of branches to remove excess snow. "But thank you."

"What are you doing, Miss Harley?"

"Just adding a few festive touches to the house. Give it a little holiday spirit."

JB adjusted his leather work glove. "Have you asked the boss? He's not real big on holidays."

"The kids told me he used to have more holiday spirit."

"It's been a few years."

"What happened?"

"He's just been a bachelor a long time. Hard to do every-thing and be happy about it."

Harley glanced down at the green fragrant branches in her arms. "You really think Mr. Sheenan will be upset that

I've spruced things up for Christmas? I'm just making some garland, adding some candles on the mantels."

He thought for a moment. "If that's all, Mr. Sheenan might be okay. But I wouldn't push him. He's not a man that likes to be bossed around."

BROCK ENTERED THE house through the kitchen door, which was how he always entered in his work clothes, but he was stopped short this afternoon by the sight of the twins hunched over the island counter carefully frosting sugar cookies that had been cut into stars and stockings, ornaments, candy canes and Christmas trees.

The kids looked up at him and smiled. Mack had flour on his cheek and Molly was licking icing from her thumb.

"Hey Dad, look what we made," Molly said. "Roll-out sugar cookies."

Brock approached the island to examine the platter filled with fanciful colors and shapes. "Nice," he said.

"Want one?" Mack asked, offering him a candy cane.

Brock shook his head. "Maybe after dinner," he answered, before looking at Harley who was drying the last of the cookie sheets. "Where did you get the cookie cutters from?" he asked her.

"Just made a paper pattern," she said.

Mack nodded. "Miss Harley made the patterns out of cardboard and we cut them all out. It took a while but it was really cool."

"You have to be careful not to roll the dough too thin," Molly explained, "and you also have to watch how much flour you use. You can't use too much or too little."

Brock's eyebrows lifted. "You got them baking today."

She blushed, her cheeks turning pink. She looked nervous as she reached for the next cookie tray. "I thought it'd be a good activity for a cold afternoon."

"Must have been a lot of work."

"It was fun."

Brock glanced back to the counter with the platter of cookies. The shapes weren't perfect and there was more frosting than cookie in some cases, but Mack and Molly looked happy. Happier than he'd seen them since returning from New York. "Maxine wouldn't let you two mess up her kitchen like this, would she?"

"But it shouldn't be Maxine's kitchen," Harley said. "It's yours, and the kids'. This is your house."

Brock frowned. "Well, let's not get too comfortable in here. She'll be back in a month and she'll want her kitchen back." He tapped each of the kids on the head. "Mack, Molly, make sure you help Miss Diekerhoff clean up. You're not to leave her with all the work."

He started for the hall, but stopped at the fireplace. A generous swag of pine covered the mantel, the green branches held in place by fat white candles.

They hadn't just been baking. They'd been decorating, too.

He slowly turned and looked back to the island counter. Mack and Molly were staring at him, waiting for his reaction.

"It smells good, doesn't it, Dad?" Mack said hopefully.

Mack glanced past the kids to Harley who appeared utterly engrossed in the glass mixing bowl she was drying so very vigorously.

He knew right away who'd been behind the green garland and candles.

"It's fine," Brock said flatly. "But let's not get carried away."

AFTER LUNCH THURSDAY, Harley prepped for dinner, creating a mustard beer bath for the two big roasts that would be tonight's dinner, and then peeled the mound of apples for tonight's apple pie.

The kids had been dashing in and out most of the day, doing chores for their dad and then entertaining themselves with various outdoor adventures.

She liked how well Mack and Molly played together. They were extremely close. Not just brother and sister, but best friends.

As Harley rolled out the pie crust and then filled each of the pie shells with the spicy apple cinnamon and sugar mixture, she thought about her daughters. They'd loved baking with her, and despite the two-and-a-half-year age difference between them, Emma and Ana had always been each other's best friend.

After carefully sliding both pies into the oven, Harley moved laundry forward, carrying folded towels upstairs and stacking the clean clothes for the ranch hands in the plastic basket that they'd come and retrieve after work tonight.

Thirty minutes later, she opened the oven door and checked on the apple pies, making sure the crusts on the pies weren't burning. The pies were browning beautifully, the flaky edges turning light gold with juice bubbling through the slits in the sugar-dusted crust.

The kitchen door flung open. "I need a Band-Aid," Mack said breathlessly. "Maybe a bunch."

Harley straightened and turned. "Everything okay?" she asked, seeing how the shoulder of his coat was powdered with snow, and something… else…. something… red.

"I think so," he said, not sounding convincing at all.

"Is that something… red on your coat?" she asked.

He looked down at his sleeve and tried to rub the red splatter off, streaking it instead.

"Where are you hurt?" she asked.

"Not me. Molly."

"Badly?"

"I don't know. She won't let me see."

Harley quickly went into the little bathroom off the kitchen, grabbed a washcloth, and then rifled through the medicine cabinet for rubbing alcohol, gauze pads, and Band-Aids. "Where is she?"

"Behind the house."

"Show me," Harley said, ignoring her coat to rush out the door.

Mack ran through the snow, with Harley close on his heels, snow crunching beneath their shoes, leading her around the side of the corral, to the back gate, where Molly was leaning against a post, her hand shielding her face as blood stained the snow around her feet.

"Dad's going to ground me for life," Mack whispered.

Harley ignored this, and bent over the girl. "Honey, it's Harley. Where are you hurt?"

"My face."

"Where on your face?"

"By my eye."

Harley's heart jumped, fell. "Let me see."

"Can't," came the muffled reply.

"Why?"

"It's bleeding too much and I don't want to get stitches."

"You might not need stitches. Faces and heads bleed a lot when they're cut. You might just need some ice. Let me see. Okay?"

Eventually, with a lot of coaxing, Harley was able to get Molly to look up and uncover her face. Blood crusted Molly's hairline and coated her temple, but as Harley gently dabbed at the gash between the girl's eyebrow and hairline, she could see that the bleeding was slowing, and the wound, maybe an inch, inch and a half, was deep but at least not to the bone.

"How did a snowball do this?" Harley asked, using her thumb to wipe away some of the blood to get a better look at the cut.

Mack didn't immediately answer.

Harley saw Molly's gaze dart to her brother.

"Um, it was a snowball fight," Mack said. "She was standing on top of the corral when I threw the snowball."

Harley glanced at the boy over her shoulder. "So she got cut when she fell?"

The kids looked at each other again. Both were making a strange face. Something was up. Harley shrugged. "You don't need to tell me. But I'm sure your dad will want to know."

"He'll kill me," Mack muttered.

"But it's my fault, too," Molly said, wincing as she touched the cut and checked her fingers for blood. "I... wanted... to play." She dabbed her head again. "And see? It's not that bad. I'm not bleeding that much now. Dad might not even notice."

"Well, let's go into the house and get you cleaned up properly," Harley said, not wanting to think about Brock's reaction, or Brock himself.

They tramped back through the snow and stomped their feet on the porch, knocking off excess snow. The back door suddenly opened and Brock was there. "Where have you been?" he demanded. "Your pies were burning."

It was only then that he noticed Molly's blood-streaked face. "Hell and damnation," he swore. "What happened?"

BROCK WALKED MOLLY into the kitchen and lifted her onto one of the kitchen stools to get a look a proper look at her face. "What happened?" he repeated.

"Snowball fight," Mack said in a small voice as Miss Diekerhoff went to the sink to wash the blood off her hands and then wet a clean cloth with warm water so he could clean Molly' face.

Brock took the warm wet cloth from the housekeeper with a gruff thanks and gently began to wipe away the blood streaks. "This cut isn't from a snowball fight," he said, shooting Mack a sharp look. "Perhaps you'd like to tell me how it happened."

The kids didn't answer and Miss Diekerhoff went to the stove to study the pies he'd pulled from the oven when he smelled the crust burning.

Her lips pursed as she prodded the blackened crust with a fork, her thick honey ponytail sliding over her shoulder, her cheeks still pink from the cold but she didn't look terribly upset. He was grateful for that. He knew the only reason the pies had burned was because she'd gone to Molly's aid.

He was grateful she had.

But he was also in need of answers. How had Molly gotten a big gash so close to her eye?

He glanced down at his daughter's face, which was still so pale the freckles popped across the bridge of her small straight nose. "So are you going to tell me what happened?" he asked, glancing from Molly to Mack, and fighting to hang on to his patience. "And how Molly got cut in a snowball fight?"

The kids just hung their heads, definitely a sign that something else had taken place. But they also weren't talking. Of course not. These two were masters of collusion. Usually Molly had the big, bright ideas and then applied pressure to her brother until he caved in, agreeing to her bold schemes. Interesting that Molly was the one hurt now. "Molly's usually the better shot," Brock added.

Mack flushed and Molly wiggled uncomfortably on the stool. "I'm out of practice," she muttered.

"Mmmm," Brock answered, pressing against the cut. It was deeper than he'd like but the edges were clean and something that could be fixed with a good butterfly bandage. No need to drive her into Marietta to the hospital. "But something tells me this wasn't an ordinary snowball fight. So what did happen?"

Neither Mack nor Molly spoke.

The housekeeper discreetly disappeared into the laundry room.

Brock waited a good minute, determined that the twins would explain what had happened.

They didn't. They kept their silence and Brock battled

his temper. He'd had enough of the twins colluding. This was why they'd been sent away to boarding school. They didn't try last year in sixth grade at their Marietta middle school. They sat in the back of the class, daydreaming and inattentive, rarely participating, and even more rarely turning in completed work. At the end of the year, the principal met with him, and recommended that Mack and Molly attend summer school to catch up on what they'd missed this year, and recommended that the twins have more structure come Fall. The twins, the principal added, were extremely bright, but highly unmotivated, more interested in their own private world than learning and applying themselves.

The twins went to summer school, kicking and screaming every day for the two intensive sessions, and then in late August, he took them by train to New York, again kicking and screaming, where he'd enrolled them at the prestigious Academy for the new school year.

The twins were upset that he left them there, but it was for their own good. They needed to be challenged, they needed to learn discipline, and they needed the study skills and good grades required for college.

But now here they were, home early, and getting into trouble. What was he going to do with them?

He surveyed their blank faces and realized they weren't going to come clean, and it just made him even angrier. Why wouldn't they listen? Why couldn't they cooperate? What was wrong with them? "So no one knows anything," he said curtly. "Fine. Don't know anything, and don't tell me. In fact, I don't think I even want to know now. I just want you two to go to bed."

"Bed?" Mack said.

"But it's not even four, Dad!" Molly cried, staring up at him in horror.

"—without dinner," Brock concluded, unmoved. "Mack, head on up. Put on your pajamas and get into bed. Molly will be up as soon as I get her bandaged up. Goodbye, and goodnight."

Mack walked out, looking beaten, and Molly was silent as Brock cleaned the wound and then used a butterfly bandage from the medicine cabinet to tightly close the cut. It should heal without a scar, but even if it did scar a bit, it wouldn't be Molly's first. Molly was definitely his wild one, while Mack was gentler and quiet, like his mom.

Brock felt a pang as he thought of Amy. His wife had only the pregnancy and then six months with the babies before she died. She never knew them, not the way he did. He wondered if she'd be disappointed in him, as a father. He wasn't a perfect father, not by any means, but he loved his kids. He loved them so much he'd sent them across the country to ensure they had the best education. He hated it when they were gone. The house was too empty. He was too empty. Life wasn't the same without them. But he had to put the kids' needs first. The prep school would get them into the best universities in the country and that's what Amy had always wanted for their children. A loving foundation, a great education, and rewarding careers. Brock was trying hard to honor Amy's dreams, but it wasn't easy.

He'd missed the kids when they were gone, and selfishly, he was glad they were back. But they weren't back for good. He'd drag them back to New York, kicking and screaming if he had to. This was for them.

And Amy.

Amy hadn't had a future. He needed to make sure her children did.

Once Molly was patched up and gone, Brock washed his hands at the sink and then dried them on a hand towel, glancing in Harley Diekerhoff's direction.

Earlier she'd lifted off the burned pastry crust from the top of the pies, throwing it away, before scooping the warn apple pie filling from inside the pie shell, transferring the golden gleaming filling into a dozen ceramic ramekins.

Now she mixed brown sugar and cinnamon and some chopped nuts with a little flour and a lot of butter, creating a crumbly brown sugar mixture.

"Making a crumble," he said, surprised, but pleased. He'd been disappointed that the pies burned. He loved apple pie. He'd wondered if one of the kids had told her it was his favorite dessert.

She nodded, and shot him a quick, shy smile. "What's the old expression? When you burn the apple pie, get rid of the crust and make a crumble?"

He lifted a brow. "I've never heard that before."

"That's strange," she said, lips twitching. "Maybe it's not an expression you use in Montana."

"Or maybe it's an expression that you just made up."

She laughed, once, and her green eyes gleamed as she suppressed the husky laugh. "Maybe I did," she admitted, beginning to sprinkle the brown sugar mixture over the first of the ramekins. "It seemed fitting, though."

He leaned against the counter and watched her work. It was strangely relaxing, watching her bake. She moved with confidence around the kitchen. She obviously liked cooking and baking, and was certainly comfortable feeding a big group. His ranch hands claimed they'd never eaten better in their lives, and it wasn't just the quantity, but the quality. Harley Diekerhoff's food actually tasted good, too.

She continued to heap topping on the ramekins and he stayed where he was, leaning against the counter, enjoying the smells of apple and cinnamon along with the roast in the oven, as well as the sight of an attractive woman moving around the kitchen.

Knowing that she'd be gone day after tomorrow made him feel less guilty for lingering.

He wasn't attached to her. Wasn't going to let his attraction interfere.

And yet she did look appealing in his kitchen, in her yellow apron with cherries and lace trim. She looked fresh and wholesome and beautiful as only a country girl could.

"You're a farm girl," he said, breaking the silence.

She paused, glanced at him. "I grew up on a dairy, and then married a dairyman."

Surprised, he said nothing for a moment, too caught off guard to know what to say. He wasn't good at conversation. It'd been too many years since he'd chatted for the hell of it. "You're divorced," he said flatly.

She sprinkled the last of the topping over the ramekins, making sure each was generously covered with brown sugar and butter before rinsing her hands. "Widowed."

He felt another strange jolt.

"I'm sorry," he said, wishing now he'd never said anything.

She dried her hands, looked at him, her features composed. "It'll be three years in February."

He shouldn't ask anything, shouldn't say anything, shouldn't continue this conversation a moment longer, not when he could see the shadows in her beautiful green eyes. But he knew loss, and what it was to lose your soul mate, and he was still moved by what she'd told him this morning, about how she'd never been able to have children, and how it'd hurt her. "How long were you married?"

"Almost twelve years."

He couldn't hide his surprise. "You must have married in high school."

"No, but I was young. I'd just turned twenty. Still had one more year of college, but Davi had graduated and we married the same weekend of his graduation ceremonies."

"A June wedding?"

"A huge, June wedding." She tried to smile. It wasn't very steady. "I think I had something like seven bridesmaids and my maid of honor."

"You met in college?"

"Yes." She turned away and began placing the ramekins on a cookie sheet. "We were both ag business majors, both from dairy families, and we grew up just eleven miles from each other."

"Your families must have been happy." He was prying now, and he knew it.

She shot him a quick glance, before sliding the cookie sheet into the hot second oven. "They weren't that happy. He was Portuguese, not Dutch. They predicted problems. They were right."

Her voice was calm, her expression serene, and yet he sensed there was so much she wasn't saying.

And yet he stopped himself from asking more. He'd already prodded Harley the way he'd prodded Molly's wound. It was time leave her alone.

"Thank you for taking care of Molly today," he said, gathering the medical supplies he'd used. "I appreciate it."

"It was nothing."

"Nothing? You lost two perfectly good pies."

She laughed. "And ended up with almost a dozen ramekins. So I think we're okay."

Brock stared at her a moment, dazzled. Her laugh was low and husky and perfectly beautiful.

She was absolutely beautiful.

Maybe too beautiful.

"Well, thanks again," he said flatly, walking out, thinking that perhaps it was a good thing that Harley was leaving the day after tomorrow.

Harley was not an easy woman to have in his house.

She made him feel things and wish for things, and he wasn't comfortable feeling and wishing. He wasn't a man who hoped for things, either. Life was hard, and the only way to survive it was to be harder. Which is why he was raising his children to be smart, tough, and honest.

He'd never coddled Mack and Molly. He'd never read them fairy tales or indulged them at Christmas with holiday fuss, impossible wish lists, or trips to see a department store Santa.

And so, yes, it was an inconvenience to change housekeepers yet again, but better to change now, before Harley Diekerhoff had them all hoping and wishing for things that couldn't be.

Chapter Five

THE RANCH HANDS devoured their beef roast and gravy, roasted potatoes, and braised root vegetables, before practically licking the little apple crisp ramekins clean, too.

Harley took the empty dishes and platters from Paul and Lewis, who brought the dishes back most nights, since they were the youngest hands, and low on the seniority totem pole.

"Everybody doing okay over there?" Harley asked, glad to see the youngsters on the doorstep, their scruffy faces ruddy from the cold. Paul and Lewis were nineteen and twenty respectively, still boys, and yet she'd discovered in her eleven days here, that these Montana boys knew how to work, and here on the ranch they certainly worked hard.

"Yes, ma'am," Lewis answered with a shy grin, pushing up the brim of his hat. "We were all just saying that you take care of us like nobody's business."

"It's my pleasure," she answered, meaning it. She'd grown fond of these shy, tough cowboys, and she'd miss them when she left Saturday. It was on the tip of her tongue to mention that she was going but then she thought better of it. It wasn't her place to break the news. Better let Brock tell them when he was ready.

"We made you something as a thank-you," Paul said, reaching behind him and lifting a large hand-tied wreath made from fragrant pine. The green wreath had been wrapped with some barbed wire and decorated with five hammered metal stars, burlap bows, and miniature pine cones.

"It's not fancy," Paul added, "not like one of those expensive ones you'd buy in Bozeman at a designer store, but we all contributed to it. See? We each made a star and signed our name to it." He pointed to a copper brown metal star in the upper left. "That's mine. Paul. And there's Lewis's, just below mine, and JB's, and the rest."

"Hope you like it," Lewis said. "And we hope you know how much we like having you here. We were also saying, if Maxine can't come back in January, maybe you could just… stay."

Both boys nodded their heads.

Harley smiled around the lump forming in her throat. "That's so lovely," she said taking the wreath and studying it in the light. "It's beautiful. Thank you. Thank all the guys, will you? I'm really touched, and pleased."

Paul blushed and dipped his head. "Glad you like it." He hesitated. "There is one other thing…" Paul hesitated again.

"Everything okay with Mr. Sheenan's kids?"

"Why do you ask?" Harley asked.

"Earlier today Lew and me caught the twins trying to cut down a tree with an ax they found in the barn. The little girl was holding the branches back so the boy could chop the trunk. We were worried something would happen, he was swinging right over her head, and told them we'd help them if they wanted to cut the tree down. They said they didn't need help so we left. But later the tree was still there, and the ax was on the ground, and we saw blood in the snow. We got worried they'd cut off their fingers or something."

Harley's stomach rose. Her heart fell. So that's how Molly got hurt. She got hit by the ax.

Brock would flip.

The kids would be in so much trouble.

She struggled to smile. "The twins are fine, but thank you so much for checking on them. If you'll tell me where they left the ax, I can go pick it up."

"No need, we already did it," Paul said. "And we finished cutting the tree down, too. We'd rather do it than see them get hurt. They're just little kids still."

Harley shut the kitchen door, wondering if she should tell Brock about the ax episode or not. He should know, but it should also be the twins who told him.

She glanced down at the beautiful rustic wreath the ranch hands had made her. It was wonderful, thoughtful, and charming and it'd actually look perfect in the kitchen, hanging on the big river rock fireplace above the mantel.

She carried the wreath toward the mantel, and was standing on tiptoe, trying to decide where the wreath would look best, when Brock entered the kitchen.

He'd changed into black plaid flannel pajama pants and a gray knit long-sleeved shirt that clung to his muscular chest and torso, before tapering to a narrow waist. "Thought I heard some of the boys," he said, glancing around.

She nodded, trying to ignore how his flannel pajamas hung from his lean hipbones, revealing several inches of bare skin and taut, toned abs between the pajama waistband and the hem of his shirt.

Her mouth dried. He had quite a hot body. Goodness knows what else all those layers of clothes hid...

She licked her upper lip, moistening it. "Lewis and Paul just left. They brought back the dishes, and this." She lifted the wreath. "The boys made it for me."

"They made you a wreath?"

She nodded, remembering how he wasn't one who liked Christmas fuss. "It's a thank-you for taking care of them."

One of his black brows lifted. "They know you're leaving then?"

She carefully placed the wreath on the seat of the rocking chair. "No."

"They just made you a wreath for the hell of it?"

"I think they like my cooking."

He made a rough sound deep in his chest. "I think they

like *you*."

"I'm not encouraging them—"

"Didn't say you were. I meant it as a compliment. They do like you, and I don't blame them for being appreciative. Maxine kept their bellies full but she didn't care too much about making them comfortable, or trying to make anyone happy. That wasn't her job." His lips curved ruefully. "Or so she'd say when the boys complained."

"I can't imagine those boys complaining about anything," she said, filling the tea kettle with water and putting it on the stove.

"They certainly didn't complain about her cooking ever again after she poured a cup of salt in their stew, and overcooked their biscuits by an hour or two, so that when the biscuits reached their table, they were hard as bricks."

Harley laughed. "She didn't!"

"She did. You don't mess with Maxine." The corners of his mouth lifted. "You eat what she cooks, you stay out of her way when she's cleaning, and you wear your clothes however you find them... wet, dry, stinking of moth balls, or smellin' of bleach."

"That sounds horrible."

"She definitely runs a tight ship. JB calls her Warden behind her back."

Harley spluttered. "As in a prison warden?"

"That's the one."

"No wonder they're hoping Maxine won't return," she

said, glancing at the kettle, waiting for it to come to a boil.

"They said that?"

She shrugged. "More or less. But it was probably just a joke—"

"It probably wasn't." He sighed, and rubbed a hand over his jaw. "I will have to do something eventually. Just not ready yet. She's known the kids since they were toddlers, and she knows her way around the place."

"So Maxine is like family to the twins."

He grimaced. "I wouldn't say that. She doesn't remember their birthday or talk much to them, but she's familiar and I trust her. She won't spoil the kids, but she won't hurt them, and she's honest to a fault. So I've put off making changes." Brock looked at her, shrugging wearily. "As you can tell, I'm not a fan of change."

No, it didn't sound like it, Harley thought.

For a moment there was just silence and then she drew a quick breath. "Speaking of the kids… have you checked on them?"

"No. Why?"

"They've been in their rooms for hours."

"They're supposed to be. I sent them to bed."

"I know, but they didn't have much lunch as they were too eager to get back outside to play—"

"If they're hungry, that's their problem, not mine."

Harley bit the inside of her lip.

But he saw her face, could read her worry. "They're in

trouble. There have to be consequences for their actions," he said.

"I know, and I agree that there must be consequences, but I don't think it'd hurt to talk to them, hear what they have to say. They've been gone for months and they only just got home."

"Then they should have made different decisions. They didn't have to go to bed without dinner. They could have told me what they were doing when Molly got hurt, because I know they were up to something. Molly didn't get hurt from a snowball fight. That was a cut next to her eye, a clean cut, with clean edges. Something made that cut and I want to know how it happened, and the kids know. But they're not talking, so they're in their room. End of story."

She nodded, wondering if now was when she should tell him what Paul and Lewis had told her, about the ax and the tree, but she didn't want to get the kids in more trouble.

"What's wrong?" Brock asked. "You think I'm too hard on them?"

The kettle whistled, saving her from immediately answering.

She grabbed a pot holder and moved the shrieking kettle to a back burner. The kettle fell silent. "Would you like a cup?" she asked, motioning to the kettle.

He shook his head. "But I am interested in your opinion. You've been here a few days with them now. Do you think I'm too hard on them?"

She squeezed the pot holder. "I'm not the best person to ask."

"Because you don't know kids?"

"Because they're your kids. I think you have to raise them according to your values."

"My brothers say I'm too hard on the twins, but they're bachelors. They don't know what it's like to have a child, to be the only one responsible for a child, never mind suddenly becoming the only person responsible for two infants still just breastfeeding when their mom is killed."

Harley couldn't imagine what it'd been like for him to bury his wife even as he had to become both mother and father to two babies. "Must have been awful," she said quietly.

"It was hell." His brow furrowed and he stared blindly across the kitchen, grief etched across his features. "Amy was such a good mom, too. She was such a natural... calm, and patient. Nothing flustered her."

"Good thing, considering you had twins."

"That was a surprise, but not a huge shock. Twins run in the Sheenan family, I have brothers who are twins—Troy and Trey—and my dad had brothers who were twins, but Amy and I were a little overwhelmed when Mack and Molly were born. They were small and needed round-the-clock feeding, and Molly had colic. She was so fussy." He smiled ruefully. "She still is."

"But Mack was easy?"

"Mack was born easy. He'd just sit there in his infant seat and chill while his sister wailed." Brock shook his head. "Thank God Mack was so good-natured. I don't think I could have handled two fussy babies on my own."

"You're a good dad," Harley said quietly, meaning it.

"I make mistakes."

"Everybody makes mistakes."

"I guess we are managing, the three of us, but I thought the hard years would be the baby years. Instead, it's getting tougher as they get older. They've got ideas and opinions and they're starting to test me—"

"They're becoming teenagers."

"They're only eleven."

"And a half." She smiled. "They told me they were born in early May. Apparently they are hoping to do something fun with you for their twelfth birthday... something about going to Orlando?"

"I have not agreed to Orlando. I would never agree to Orlando. Flathead Lake, yes. Florida, no."

"Why not Orlando?" she asked.

"Too many people. Don't like crowds. Not a big fan of amusement parks."

"Have you ever been to an amusement park?"

"No."

"You can't blame them for being curious."

"They're Montana kids. They're just as happy camping and fishing. So if they really want to go somewhere for their birthday, I'll take them to Flathead Lake. Amy's parents have a cabin there and we can fish and hike."

"Molly fishes?"

"For their tenth birthday I gave each of them new poles and tackle."

Harley squashed her smile. She couldn't imagine her Emma or Ana ever being excited about a fishing pole and tackle, but her girls were good athletes and had loved skiing and snowboarding and having adventures with their dad. That's how they'd died, too. Setting off on an adventure with their dad.

David should have never taken off in that bad weather. Never, never, ever.

But he never did listen to her. He was always so sure he knew what was best.

Her smile faded.

She realized Brock had stopped talking and was looking at her. "What are you thinking about?" he asked.

She shook her head, unable to talk about the kids, or how they died, or how selfish their father had been, piloting his own plane when there had been severe weather warnings.

"Nothing," she whispered, pushing back the flood of memories, heartsick all over again. Emma and Ana and Davi, her little boy. Gone. All gone.

She turned to the cabinet, stared blindly at the boxes of tea, waiting for her vision to clear.

"I'm sorry," Brock said, after a moment. "I forgot that

this is a difficult subject for you."

"It's okay," she said thickly. She turned to face him a few moments later. "I'm sure you know it, but you're lucky. You have such sweet, smart kids. You should be proud."

"I'd be prouder if they didn't run away from school and if they'd tell me the truth when one of them gets hurt."

"Maybe they're scared that if they tell you the truth they'll get in trouble."

"I've never hit them. There's no reason for them to be afraid of me."

Harley regarded him a moment, still feeling the ache of grief that accompanied thoughts of her children. "Maybe they just need you to talk to them more. Reassure them that they can trust you—"

"Of course they can trust me. I'm their father."

"You can be a little intimidating," she said gently, thinking that right now he looked about as soft and receptive as the granite counter slabs in the kitchen. "Maybe just try to talk to them as a friend."

His big arms crossed over his chest, drawing the knit shirt tight at his shoulders, revealing those hard carved abs again. "I'm not here to be their friend."

Suddenly JB's words came to Harley's mind. *Mr. Sheenan's been a bachelor too long.* Is that what this was?

She dropped her voice, softening her tone. "Don't you want to know who they are? Don't you want to know about their ideas... their feelings... their dreams?"

His upper lip curled. His expression was openly mocking. "For a woman who never had kids, you certainly seem to have a lot of opinions on how to raise them."

She flinched, caught off guard.

She shouldn't have been caught off guard, though. She'd pushed, wanting to help, but her attempt had backfired, and he'd lashed out at her instead.

It was a good lesson. Not just because he'd hurt her feelings, but because she wasn't a counselor, a family member, or a friend. She was his employee and day after tomorrow she'd be gone.

Dropping the teabag in her mug, Harley vowed to mind her own business until then.

She counted to ten as she filled her mug with hot water, and then counted to ten again.

When she was confident she could speak calmly, she faced Brock. "I never said I'd never had kids. I said I don't have children *now*." She looked Brock in the eye, held his gaze. "My children died with their father in a small plane crash three years ago February. And maybe you don't need to be friends with your kids, but I loved being friends with mine."

Blinking back tears, she grabbed her mug and headed to her room to sip tea and read in bed and think of anything and everything besides her children who were angels now.

BROCK CURSED UNDER his breath as Harley disappeared.

He'd hurt her again and he hadn't meant to hurt her as much as get her to stop, back off. He wasn't accustomed to being lectured, and she'd given him an earful and he'd had enough of her dispensing advice.

He didn't need advice, not when it came to parenting his children. Mack and Molly were his kids and he was raising them the way he thought best.

But with Harley gone from the kitchen, he could still feel her surprise and hurt. He could still see the bruised look in her eyes when she'd turned away.

Shit.

This is exactly why he didn't date and avoided polite society. He didn't fit in polite society. He was better away from people, better on his own.

Angry with himself, he went to the barn to do his nightly check before bed. As he entered the barn, his dogs were immediately at his heels and followed him from stall to stall as he greeted each horse, stroking noses, giving treats, trying not to think about Harley or what she'd told him.

She'd been a mother. She'd had kids. Her children had died.

He cringed all over again, disgusted with himself, not just for his put-down, but for his need to put her in her place.

What was wrong with him?

Why did he have to shame a woman?

If his mom were alive she'd be horrified. She'd raised her

boys to be gentlemen. She'd taught her five sons that women were equals and deserving of protection and respect.

He certainly hadn't been respectful to Harley tonight.

Heart heavy, he returned to the house, locked up the doors, and turned off unnecessary lights but he couldn't settle down in front of the TV, not when his conscience smacked him for being a heel.

Brock climbed the stairs two by two, and then the narrow staircase to the third floor bedroom he'd carved from the attic.

He knocked on the closed door with a firm rap of his knuckles.

She opened the door after a long moment, peeking out from behind the door. Her long hair was loose, a thick golden brown curtain about her face, and from behind the door he glimpsed a bare shoulder, her skin creamy and smooth.

She must have been changing when he'd knocked.

Just like that, his body hardened, pulse quickening.

He wanted her and he couldn't remember when he'd lasted wanted anyone.

"I didn't know," he said shortly, glaring down at her, now unhappy with himself for being unable to manage the way he responded to her. In the eleven years since Amy died he'd never had an issue with lusting or physical desire, but something about Harley annihilated his famous self-control. "And I'm sorry. I'm sorry for being rough with you and not being more… sensitive. As you might have noticed, I'm not a very sensitive guy."

"I share the blame," she said. "I shouldn't have been offering advice. I won't do it again."

They were the right words but somehow they didn't make him feel better.

"Why didn't you tell me you had kids?"

"It's not something I talk about anymore." She tugged her robe up, over her shoulder, concealing her delectable skin. "I've discovered that people treat you differently if they know. *She's the lady who lost her husband and three children…* I could hear people whisper that, or look at me with pity, and I've found that it's just better for people not to know. That way there's no awkwardness." She made another little adjustment before stepping from behind the door, firmly tying her sash at her waist. "Which is why I didn't want you to know I had children. I liked coming here to work knowing that my past didn't matter, that my grief was my grief alone, and that this Christmas I'd get through the holidays with a minimum of fuss."

"And then my kids came home," he said quietly.

"Your eleven-year-olds." Her lips curved but her expression was haunted. "My oldest was eleven when she died." She drew a slow breath. "Eleven is such a great age, too."

Brock could see how hard she was trying to keep it together, trying to be calm and strong, and her strength and courage moved him far more than tears ever could.

He'd wanted her moments ago because she was beautiful and desirable and now he just wanted to hold her to comfort her.

But he couldn't.

There was no way he could make a move, not even to comfort. She was his employee. He was responsible for her.

"Tell me about your kids," he said.

Her head dipped. Her voice dropped. "It's hard to talk about them. Hurts."

He heard her voice crack and his chest grew tight. It was all he could do to not reach out and caress her cheek. "It doesn't help to talk about them?"

Her head shook and she lifted her head, looked up at him, eyes bright. "I'm still mad they're gone. I don't know why they're gone."

It was the tear trembling on her lower lashes that did him in.

He reached out to wipe the tear from her lashes and then the tear from the other side and when he couldn't catch the tears because they were falling too fast he did the only thing he could think of. He drew her toward him and kissed her.

The kiss wasn't meant to be sexual, and her lips were cool and they trembled beneath his. Brock was afraid he'd scared her, but then she slowly kissed him back, the coolness of her mouth giving away to a simmering heat.

He liked the way she kissed him back, her lips opening to him, and he took her mouth, craving her warmth. She tasted both sexy and sweet and he drank her in, feeling more than he wanted to feel, feeling more than he ever expected to feel and he leaned into her, backing her against the doorframe, his big body pressed to hers, needing to get as close as he could.

HARLEY DIDN'T UNDERSTAND the kiss, only that it was fierce and real, and it opened something inside of her, something blistering, and dangerous, because it silenced her brain and muted all thought.

Suddenly there was nothing but this moment, this man, this kiss.

There was no past, no future.

Nothing but this wild need burning inside her.

The wild need was unlike anything she'd ever felt, maybe because it wasn't about a particular sensation, but all sensation. She needed to feel and feel and feel because it'd been forever since she felt anything but cold, and anger, and pain.

The rational Harley would have stopped him at a kiss, but the rational Harley was gone. This other Harley was in her place, wanting the kiss, wanting his hands, wanting his knee pressing up where she was so very warm.

She arched against him and kissed him back, craving everything he could give her. She'd felt nothing for so long and now this... this inferno, need so great she didn't think she'd ever get enough.

He devoured her mouth, his tongue plunging in, stroking, teasing. Her hands rose to his chest and she clung to him, legs weak, heart pounding. His hand tugged at her robe, pulling it open, exposing her breasts. He lifted his head briefly to gaze down at her, and his dark hot gaze so carnal hungry that she felt as though she were melting.

"You're beautiful," he groaned, head dropping to kiss her again, as he cupped one of her breasts, fingers playing her taut nipple as if he'd known her body forever.

In a strange way she felt as if she'd known him forever, too, and she would have given him everything, and all of her, but a shout came from below.

"Dad! *Dad!* Where are you?"

Brock reluctantly lifted his head. Harley felt a pang as he shifted back.

"Molly," he said, as the girl continued to shout his name.

"Dad, if we promise never ever to be stupid again, can we please have some dinner?"

Molly's wail was both funny and quirky and sweet, just like the girl herself and just like that, reality returned, practically slapping Harley across the face.

What in God's name was she doing?

Brock took a reluctant step back and dragged a hand through his black hair. "Bad timing," he muttered.

"Maybe it's good timing," Harley answered, legs trembling. She'd come so close to losing her head. She'd come so close to losing control…

Shocked and more than a little mortified, Harley dragged

the edges of her robe closed. Face hot, cheeks flaming she moved inside her room. "Go to her," she said. "I'll see you tomorrow." And then before he could say a word, she closed the door as fast as she could.

Chapter Six

B ROCK STOOD IN the middle of Molly's room, grimly listening to the twins recount their tree-chopping adventure, grinding his jaw to keep from expressing horror when he realized just how close his daughter had come to losing an eye… or worse.

"That was as stupid as you could get," he said bluntly, giving his children a severe look as they sat side by side on Molly's bed. "And so damn dangerous—"

"I know," Mack agreed. "I can't believe I let Molly talk me into it."

Brock made a rough sound of disapproval. "Don't blame your sister. That's pathetic, Mack. It is. You have a brain. Use it."

The boy nodded, gaze dropping but Molly stared back at her father. "We wouldn't have to do it if you'd get us a tree," she said, expressing little of the remorse she'd shown when he'd first entered her room fifteen minutes ago.

"That's absurd," Brock snorted "You can't blame me for

nearly losing your eye… or your head."

"Why won't you let us have a tree?" she persisted indignantly.

"We have real live trees growing outside. We don't need to cut one and bring it inside."

"Why not? They're pretty," Molly flashed. "And everybody has one. We want one, too."

"Well, sneaking off with an ax into the woods isn't the way to get one."

"Then how do we get one if you won't chop one down for us?" Molly demanded.

Brock was losing his temper. "I'm not discussing Christmas trees now."

"But you never do. You never discuss anything we want to talk about. You just make up all these rules and expect us to follow them—"

"Yes," he interrupted. "That's right. I do. You're the kids. I'm the adult. I make the rules. You obey. See how that works?"

"But your rules don't make sense," she protested under her breath.

"Of course they do," he snapped.

"Maybe to you, but not to us. Some of your rules are just… mean."

"Mean?"

Her head nodded, her lips pressing flat. "It's like you're the Grinch and you hate Christmas—"

"The *Grinch*?"

She nodded again. "You can't stand for anyone to play or have fun. You hate it when we want to do something fun. Sometimes I think you don't even love us!"

Brock's jaw dropped. "*What*?"

"Maybe you even hate us!" she flung at him, scrambling off the bed and running to the adjoining bathroom where she slammed the door closed.

Brock stared at the bathroom door in disbelief before turning to Mack, who sat very still on the edge of his sister's bed.

Mack glanced up at his dad and then looked down again at his hands which were knotting unhappily in his lap.

Brock's heart pounded as if he'd just run through very deep snow. "Is she being dramatic or does she really feel this way?"

Mack's head hung lower.

Brock suppressed the queasy sensation in his gut. Did his kids really think he hated them? "Tell me the truth, Mack."

"I don't want to speak for her."

Brock studied his son's thin slumped shoulders and the curve of his neck. Mack had never been a big, sturdy kid, but he looked downright skinny at the moment. "Then don't speak for her, speak for yourself. How do you feel? Do you really think I don't love you?"

"I know you love us," Mack said in a low voice. He hesitated a long moment. "But..." His voice faded away. He didn't finish the sentence.

"But what?"

"But sometimes you seem so… annoyed…by us. Like we're a pain and always in your way—"

"*No.*"

Mack shrugged. "Okay."

His son's half-hearted response made Brock want to hit something, throw something, which wasn't probably the right response. Brock drew a breath, and then another, trying to be patient, trying to understand when he couldn't understand at all. He'd never dated anyone after their mother in order to protect and preserve Amy's memory. He'd refused to spoil them so his kids would be raised with solid family values. And he'd only sent his kids away to school recently when it became clear that they needed to be pushed, socially, academically, if they were to succeed.

Brock crossed his arms, hiding his hard fists. "Don't say okay just to placate me, Mack. You can speak up, have an opinion."

The boy slumped even more unhappily. "I don't want to make you mad. I don't like making you mad."

"You don't have to be scared of me," Brock retorted.

Mack looked up at him, worry in his dark eyes. "But you are kind of scary when you're mad."

Brock couldn't believe what he was hearing. Dumbfounded, he stared at his boots, unable to think or speak. Were his kids really afraid of him? His gut churned. "Mack,

I've never hit you. Never even spanked you. How can you be afraid of me?"

Mack's shoulders lifted and fell. "You don't smile or laugh or do fun stuff with us. You just get mad at us. A lot."

Brock closed his eyes at the rush of words. It was a lot to take in. Hard to process it all. He exhaled slowly. "So I don't do fun stuff, and just get mad. Is that it?"

Mack nodded.

Brock felt like punching something. Instead he drew a deep breath, trying hard to sort out everything he was hearing. "Can you explain the *stuff?* What stuff are you missing out on?"

"Everything. Going to the movies and having friends over and taking trips together somewhere fun. The only time you've ever taken us anywhere was when you took us to boarding school."

Molly opened the bathroom door to shout. "And Christmas! We don't ever have Christmas or Valentine's Day or Easter or Fourth of July. We don't do holidays or anything fun because you don't believe in fun. It's against your religion apparently."

Brock clapped a hand on his head thinking his brain was going to explode. "That's ridiculous. You are both being ridiculous. Knock it off and grow up. You're eleven, almost twelve—" he stopped midsentence, hearing himself.

Grow up.

He'd just told his eleven-year-olds to grow up. It's what

his dad always used to say to him and look how close he and his dad were today....

Brock exhaled slowly. If Amy were here, she'd be disgusted with him. If Amy were here...

... none of this would be happening.

The kids would have Christmas and Valentine's Day and all the other days. They'd laugh and play because Amy believed in laughing and playing.

That's why he'd fallen in love with Amy. She made him want to laugh and play and without her....

Without her, life was just hard. He missed her. He needed her. Not just for her laughter, but for her support.

Raising two kids was hard.

Brock had been doing it a long time on his own but God help him, he was tired and lonely and alone.

He swallowed with difficulty, aware that the twins were staring at him, anxious and worrying about what would happen next.

His eyes burned. His chest ached. He loved his children, he did, but he was beginning to realize his love might just not be enough.

"Go down and get a snack if you're hungry," he said quietly. "I'll see you in the morning."

IN BED, IN her room, Harley heard almost every word.

She didn't want to hear but her room was just above Molly's and the voices carried far too easily in the air duct.

She couldn't remember when she last felt so conflicted.

The kiss… shouldn't have happened. But oh, the kiss, it'd been amazing. And she shouldn't be thinking about Brock, or feeling sorry for him, or the kids. She shouldn't be involved and she shouldn't care.

But she did.

She didn't want to worry about them, but she felt so terribly protective.

It was a mistake coming here. It was a mistake getting attached. She was so very attached.

Leaving would hurt so much.

And she was leaving the day after tomorrow.

Harley closed her eyes, drew a deep breath, trying to block out her thoughts, her feelings about returning to her family.

She couldn't. She wasn't ready to return to California.

A knock sounded on her door.

Harley left her bed, slipped her robe on over her nightgown and opened the door.

Mack stood in the hall with a plate of yesterday's sugar cookies and a glass of milk. "We brought you a snack." He smiled at her and yet his dark eyes looked anxious. "We hope you didn't get in trouble with Dad."

Harley took the cookies and milk. "Thank you for thinking of me, and no, I didn't get in trouble with your dad."

"He's not really as scary as he seems," Mack said under his breath.

"I don't think he is scary at all."

"You don't?"

She shook her head, smiling. "No. I think he's just tired and a little bit lonely. I have a feeling he still misses your mom."

"She died when we were babies. We didn't even know her."

"But your dad loved your mom, and every time he looks at you, he thinks of her." Harley set the cookies and milk on her nightstand. "He loved her a lot."

Mack shrugged. "That's what he says."

"You don't believe him?"

"Oh I believe him. But I kind of wish he didn't love her so much."

Harley blinked. "Why?"

"Because maybe then Dad would have married someone else and we would have had a mom."

Oh.

Oh, baby boy.

Harley's heart ached. Here he was, eleven years old and wondering what it would have been like to have a mom.

She reached for Mack and gave him a swift hug. These kids were stealing her heart, bit by bit, piece by piece. "Don't give up hope," she whispered in his ear before releasing him.

His eyes watered as he looked up at her. "I won't."

HARLEY WENT DOWNSTAIRS the next morning at five-thirty.

It was the time she started her day but when she reached the kitchen the lights were already on, the coffee made, and the fire burning brightly in the big fireplace, which meant that Brock was up already. She wondered if one of the cows had been calving, or if he was just taking care of paperwork.

At six he walked through the kitchen to refill his coffee. She was making a breakfast casserole and she kept chopping the ham and Swiss cheese, trying to appear nonchalant but her pulse was racing in her veins and she wanted him to say something to help her make sense of what happened last night. That kiss had been so hot and intense… and so damn confusing, too.

She hadn't slept well, tossing and turning, playing the kiss over and over in her head, all the while wondering what he'd say or do this morning. Now it was morning and she just needed to know if he was angry, disappointed, or maybe just regretful.

She dumped the cheese and meat into a bowl and started dicing the green onion.

"Harley."

She looked up to see Brock at the island, hands on the counter.

She set the knife down on the cutting board. "Yes?"

"Did you in any way encourage the kids to go chop down their own Christmas tree?"

Harley wiped her hands on the skirt of her apron. "No."

"You didn't know they were tree hunting?"

"No."

"And if I told you I didn't approve of all this Christmas fuss, and didn't want them to get caught up in any more fuss, what would you say?"

"I'd ask you to let us have one more fun day of fuss before I leave tomorrow."

"But you wouldn't go behind my back? You wouldn't do something I wouldn't approve of?"

"No." Harley reached for the knife and the loaf of French bread. "I wouldn't do that. I couldn't do that." She turned the bread and began slicing. "I don't believe in breaking up families, and it would devastate me if I came between you and your kids."

Brock stared at her a long moment. "You were married twelve years."

"Almost twelve years."

"Did you like being married?"

She paused slicing, her knife suspended in mid-air. She didn't know how to answer that. She'd liked parts of marriage. Parts of it had been so hard. She hadn't expected all the arguing. They'd fought over everything. Mainly money, and then family, sex, control. But always about money. He didn't like budgets and saving. She'd been raised to be frugal, raised to bank your money, not spend it.

And then the discovery that David wanted out. He'd fallen in love with someone else.

"We were separated at the time my husband and kids

died," Harley said quietly, turning the loose bread slices sideways to cut them into strips. "No one knew that we were struggling. At least, I'd never told anyone in my family that David wanted a divorce. I couldn't." She looked up at Brock. "I didn't want a divorce. Maybe it wasn't a perfect marriage, but it was my marriage, and David was my husband, and we had three beautiful children. And I lost it all because he went behind my back, ignored me." She gave her head a small shake and returned to cubing the bread. "So no, I would never defy you. Not unless it was life and death."

Brock's dark head inclined. "Thank you," he said quietly.

HARLEY WORKED HARD to stay busy all day, and worked even harder to stay out of Brock's way, so when the kids were at loose ends in the early afternoon, and Harley had caught up on her chores, she bundled up in layers and headed outside to find the kids, her pockets full of carrots and charcoal briquettes and an extra scarf to help them build a snowman.

At first the twins laughed at her, claiming they were too old to make snowmen, but when Harley started rolling snow around to make a big snow ball, they suddenly joined in, competing to see who could make the biggest ball and before she knew it, they were throwing snow and pushing each other into snow and chasing each other around the yard.

Harley screamed with laughter as Molly shoved a glove full of snow down the back of her coat, and inside her shirt.

"That's cold," she shrieked, dancing from foot to foot as she swiped at the snow, trying to get it out.

The snow wasn't going to come out. It was already melting and making her wet and cold, which meant the only thing left to do was give Molly a taste of her own medicine.

Harley made a big snow ball, ducked behind one of the pine trees and waited until Molly was whizzing snow balls at Mack and then dropped her snow ball right on top of Molly's head.

But instead of laughing, Molly fell apart and stormed off, marching into the house.

Harley felt bad when Molly left. "I shouldn't have done that," she said, brushing snow from her gloves.

"You were just playing."

"She didn't like it."

"Molly likes to make the rules and be in charge. If she's not, she has a hissy fit."

Harley shot him a quick side glance. "Does that bother you?"

"Most of the time, no. Every now and then, yeah. She doesn't realize that she wins because I let her win. I just don't care enough to always fight."

"That's very mature of you."

He shrugged. "It's just a survival thing. Uncle Troy always said you got to pick your fights or you'll be like Uncle Trey, serving time for fighting the wrong folks." Mack saw her shocked expression and grimaced. "Yeah. I know. It's bad."

"This is your dad's brother?"

"Yeah, and Uncle Trey was our favorite uncle, too. He used to live in Marietta so we'd see him a lot. But he's been in jail a long time now." Mack added a note of warning. "But don't mention it to my dad. It makes him really upset. Uncle Trey was like Dad's best friend."

The wind swept through the trees, blowing snow from the limbs as they started walking back to the house.

Mack peeled off his gloves wet and tugged off his hat. "I get mad at Molly sometimes," he said, "but she is my best friend."

Harley smiled. "You're lucky you have each other."

He nodded. "Yeah. But it's going to be weird in January."

Harley glanced at the boy. "Weird, why?"

"Because I don't know what's going to happen with the Academy." They'd reached the back porch and took turns scraping snow off the soles of their boots. "I don't want to go back, not without her."

"But Molly's going back—" Harley broke off, seeing Mack's brow furrow and his eyes darken. "Isn't she?"

"They kicked her out." Mack's lips compressed. "Permanently, this time."

"What did she do?"

He sighed. "Everything."

Harley shivered inside her coat. "She's been in trouble

before?"

"Yes. They warned her that next time they'd expel her, but that's what Molly wanted. She doesn't like being away from Dad. She thinks Dad needs us here, home, so she... acts out. Does stupid stuff." His dark head lifted, his hair shaggy and thick like his father, his dark eyes his father's too. "She's not bad, though. She just gets so homesick." His shoulders twisted. "I do, too."

Harley heard the dogs bark in the distance. Brock must be heading toward the house. "Your dad doesn't know, does he?" she asked.

"No."

"He needs to know."

"Yeah. But I don't know how to tell him. He'll just get mad." Mack sighed, expression troubled. "Seems like he's always so mad."

"I think your dad doesn't know how to handle the fact that you and Molly are growing up. I also think he's worried that he's going to make a mistake as a dad, and do the wrong thing."

"The mistake was sending us to the Academy."

"It won't get any easier by not telling him. Better to break the news and get it over with. You'll feel better when you tell him."

He grimaced. "I don't think so."

She laughed and ruffled his hair which was icy cold. "He loves you, both you and Molly, so much. You have to believe that. You have to give him a chance. Now let's go in and get into dry clothes, then you find Molly, make sure she's okay, and I'll start making some hot cocoa. Sound like a plan?"

SHE WAS AT the stove, monitoring the milk in the saucepan when footsteps sounded on the back porch and Brock entered the kitchen.

"I'm making the kids hot chocolate," she said, skin prickling as Brock approached the stove, glanced down into the pan. "Would you like some?"

"Hot chocolate?" he repeated.

"Yes, with marshmallows and whipped cream and chocolate shavings." She smiled at him, feeling nervous and shy. She'd shared an awful lot this morning and now she wished she hadn't. Only thing to do now was keep it professional. "Or I can keep it simple. Just cocoa if you prefer."

"I'll take some whipped cream," he said, adding a log to the fire before dropping onto one of the stools at the counter. "If it's not too much trouble."

She felt her cheeks warm. "It's not too much trouble." She checked the milk to make sure it hadn't started to boil and then retrieved another mug. After burning the pies yesterday she didn't want to scald the milk today. But it would be a lot easier to concentrate if Brock were somewhere else.

"Want to call the kids?" she asked, staring down at the simmering milk, gauging the tiny bubbles.

"No."

She glanced at him over her shoulder. He practically filled the island, his big arms resting on the counter, his shoulders squared. "The cocoa is going to be ready soon."

"But it's not ready yet," he said mildly.

"It will be *soon*."

"Soon, but not yet."

She glared at him. "You're being difficult."

"According to my kids I'm always difficult. And mean. And determined to make them unhappy for the rest of their lives."

She hadn't meant to laugh. She hadn't even known she was going to laugh but the gurgle of laughter slipped from her and she clapped a hand over her mouth to stifle the sound.

"It's not funny," he said, and yet his eyes were smiling at her.

"No, it's not." Her lips twitched as she took in his big strong body, his black gleaming hair and his dark eyes in that ruggedly handsome face. "I'm sorry."

"You don't sound sorry at all."

Her lips twitched again. "I'm trying to sound sympathetic."

"You're not trying very hard."

"I'm also trying not to tell you I told-you-so."

"Again, not trying very hard."

She bit down into her lip to check her smile, and yet he

was smiling a little, a small sexy smile that made her heart turn over and her insides melt.

He was too good-looking when he smiled. Much, much too good-looking.

"Don't do that," she said, trying to sound severe.

"Do what?"

"Be all friendly and sexy—"

"Sexy?" he pounced on the word, black eyebrows rising.

"Because from now on we are keeping things professional."

"Professional," he repeated.

Her tummy flipped and her pulse quickened. "Platonic."

He said nothing just looked at her from beneath his dark lashes, his expression lazy, sultry, knowing.

He remembered how she'd kissed him last night. He remembered how she responded.

Harley flushed. "I'm here to do a job and that's the only reason I'm here—"

"Harley—"

"I'm serious. I'm the housekeeper and cook—"

He was up off the stool and at her side, yanking the sauce pan with the boiling milk from the hot burner even as the milk bubbled up and over the edge of the pan all over the stove.

"Damn," Harley cried. She could tell from the scorched smell that she hadn't just wasted the milk, she'd burned the pan. She looked up at Brock and jabbed a finger in his chest as he was standing far too close. "This is your fault. None of this would have happened if you'd just gotten the kids like I told you."

BROCK STARED DOWN into Harley's bright green eyes, seeing the sparkle of anger that made her eyes light up and her cheeks flush. He liked this side of her, feisty and fierce, her finger pressed to his chest as she took him to task.

He'd always admired intelligent women, and Amy had been one of the smartest girls at Marietta High School, testing off the charts, and earning several full-ride scholarships to prestigious universities. But Amy hadn't wanted to leave Montana. She loved Montana and Brock too much to leave either, so Brock and Amy both attended school in Bozeman, earning degrees together, graduating together and settling down on their new ranch, with Brock to work the ranch and Amy to work in Marietta in the commercial banking division for Copper Mountain Savings & Loan. She'd been on her way to work when her car was broadsided.

One of the neighbors, a fellow rancher, was first on the scene and the neighbor called Brock. Brock made it to Amy before the paramedics, and he was with her at the scene when she died. There hadn't been time to transport her anywhere, and so Brock was always grateful he'd reached her quickly, grateful he'd been able to kiss her and promise to always take care of the babies, and raise them properly.

He didn't know if she'd heard him. He didn't know if

she'd understood what he was saying, but in the eleven years since she'd died, he'd kept his promise to her. He'd always put the kids first, which meant he didn't date or go out with friends, or screw around with his brothers.

No, he'd stayed here, on the ranch, focusing on work and the kids.

At times it'd been damn lonely. But Amy was the love of his life and impossible to replace. He hadn't wanted to replace her, either.

But being alone for so long had made him a harder man. He knew he was tougher, colder, less affectionate than he'd been when Amy was alive. Amy had been good for him. She'd been his laughter, his best friend, his sunshine.

Staring down now into Harley's face Brock keenly felt the loss of laughter and sunshine.

It'd been eleven years since he'd had a partner. He could use a best friend again.

Brock reached out and captured Harley's finger, gently bending the finger, shaping her hand into a fist, covering her fist with his own.

Her hand was warm and small, her skin soft.

He liked touching her. Hell, he'd like to touch all of her. Celibacy had lost its appeal a long time ago. "We need to talk about last night, what happened upstairs," he said.

He saw a flicker in her eyes before she dropped her gaze. "No, we don't," she whispered.

"We do," he answered, wanting to kiss her again, needing to kiss her again, but not comfortable bedding her as long as she worked for him. But at the same time, once she left here tomorrow he didn't know where she was going to go or what she planned on doing. "Tomorrow your replacement comes."

"Yes."

"Are you flying back to California, or staying in Marietta?"

"I haven't thought that far."

"Do you even know where you're going tomorrow?"

"No."

The twins suddenly raced into the kitchen, pushing each other as they rounded the corner. They skidded to a halt as they spotted him holding Harley's hand.

HARLEY SAW THE kids' expression as they saw their dad holding her hand and she broke free, moving quickly to the sink. "Just a little burn," she said briskly, turning the faucet on and running her hand beneath the water. "It'll be fine."

Brock lounged against the counter. "You're sure you don't want ice?"

She shot him a swift glance. "It's fine," she said flatly. "But I do need to get a new pan and start fresh milk if we want that hot chocolate anytime soon."

"Or maybe we just forget the hot chocolate," Brock said casually, "and go into town for dinner and a movie."

The twins looked at him, wide eyed. "But you *hate* movies," Molly said.

"And eating in town," Mack added.

Brock frowned. "I don't *hate* movies or dinner out. We just don't ever have a lot of time so we don't go into Marietta much, but I thought it'd be fun to go tonight—"

"Fun?" Molly screwed her face up in horror. "Did you just say fun? Who are you? And where did my dad go?"

"Never mind," Brock said, shrugging. "We can just stay here. Have a quiet night at home—"

"No!" Mack said.

Molly ran to Brock and flung her arms around his waist, squeezing him tight. "Just teasing, Dad. Come on, laugh. Take a joke. We want to go. We do!"

Brock's lips curved in a crooked smile as he glanced from his daughter to his son and back. "I have a very good sense of humor. I have to, with you two for children." Then he stroked Molly's hair, smoothing the reddish-brown strands. "And of course I love you. I've loved you from the moment your mom and I found out we had a baby on the way. Now get your coats and I'll see what's playing at The Palace tonight."

THE KIDS WENT to get their coats, leaving Brock and Harley alone in the kitchen. "I'm glad you're taking them out," Harley said, happy with Brock for making an effort to do something the kids would enjoy. She was also proud of him for putting his feelings into words. Kids needed to hear that they were loved. Actions were important, but words were essential, too. "You will have fun."

"So will you," he answered, looking up from his cell phone, as he'd immediately gone online to check for movie times. "Do you care what movie we see? Or are you up for anything?"

Harley's mouth opened, closed. A lump filled her throat. "I can't go," she said quietly, going to the stove to retrieve the burnt pan. "This is a Dad and kids thing."

"But the kids like you and I know they'd enjoy having you along—"

"No." Harley's voice was firm. "They might like me, but they *need* you. They need time alone with you, being your primary focus, getting your undivided attention."

"But they've always been my focus. They've never had competition. It's always been the three of us."

"Good." She smiled at him, liking him even more for wanting to include her, but she wasn't part of the family. She was the temporary housekeeper and cook and leaving in the morning. "You go. I'll manage things here and I'm happy managing things here. I love that you're taking the kids out and doing fun things. It's not just your kids who need to play. You need to play, too, Brock Sheenan. You're a good man. You deserve a good life."

He was quiet a moment, staring out the window. "Don't leave tomorrow."

Her heart turned over. "I have to."

"Why?"

"You know why."

"Because it's hard to be around kids," he said.

"Being around kids makes me miss being a mom." She swallowed hard. "Makes me… envious… of what I don't have." She looked at him, wanting him to understand. "If your kids were awful or hateful it'd be easier here. I could cook and clean and leave in January without a second thought. But your kids remind me of m—" she broke off, pressed a hand to her mouth to keep the word in.

Mine.

The twins needed a mother, too, and she knew how to mother. She'd been a good mother and if she weren't careful, she'd want to stay here. She'd want to take care of the kids, spoiling them, hugging them. They were good kids. Lovely kids. They needed to be cherished. Adored.

I could love them, she thought, looking at Brock. *I could love them, and you…*

Harley turned back to the sink, and turned the hot water on, filling the scalded pan. "Go," she said hoarsely. "*Please.*"

Chapter Seven

HARLEY WAS IN bed reading when Brock and the kids returned from their dinner and movie night in Marietta. It was late, past ten, which meant they had made quite a night of it. She hoped they'd had dinner, seen the movie, and then gone somewhere for ice cream or dessert after. It's what she would have done with her kids.

She listened as voices and footsteps sounded on the stairs. The kids sounded giddy, silly, their voices were louder than usual and animated. She smiled to herself, listening, catching only bits and pieces of their conversation, warmed by their laughter, happy that they were happy.

Book pressed to her chest, she listened to Brock's heavier footsteps echo in the stairwell below. It sounded as if he was in hallway outside the kids rooms talking to them. One of the twins must have said something funny because suddenly she heard his laugh, deep and rich and so incredibly sexy she felt a fizz of pleasure.

He didn't laugh often but when he did it was so damn

appealing. He was so appealing. She was falling for him.

That's why she wasn't cold and frozen anymore.

That's why her heart tingled and her body felt so sensitive.

She was coming to life again. She was waking up, feeling, and it scared her. But she couldn't stop the prickling, tingling sensation creeping through her, sensation in her fingers and toes, sensation surging into her arms and legs, into her torso, where she'd been so cold for so long, and she wasn't cold anymore.

Her heart still hurt, but it wasn't the icy pain of old, but a new flutter of emotion, a strange bewildering flutter that was fear and yet excitement.

Exhilaration.

As well as dread.

She was feeling and needing and wanting and yet she didn't want to be hurt again, wasn't ready to be hurt again.

Harley took a quick breath, and left the bed and began to pack. It wouldn't take long to pack, she hadn't brought that much with her from California, but at least emptying the closet and the dresser drawers would give her something to do.

Activity would keep her from thinking too much. She didn't want to think too much, not tonight, not when she was battling her heart, trying to keep it under control.

She had to be smart. Had to be practical. She didn't belong here, not long term, and she couldn't forget herself and invest in a family that wasn't her own, and risk having her heart broken all over again.

A hesitant knock sounded on the bedroom door. The door opened and Molly stuck her head around the edge of the door. "Miss Diekerhoff?"

Harley closed the suitcase. "Yes, Molly?"

"I wanted to apologize… for earlier. I was kind of bratty outside, when we had the snowball fight. I'm sorry."

"You were fine."

But Molly shook her head. "No. I was rude. I know I was rude and you've done so many nice things for Mack and me and I want you to know I appreciate it."

"I haven't done anything."

"Well, compared to Maxine you've been amazing."

Harley smiled and sat down on the foot of the bed. "Maxine sounds very… interesting."

"Oh, she is. She's… interesting… all right." The girl smiled and glanced past Harley to the suitcase on the floor. "You're packing."

It was a statement, not a question, and Harley felt a pang. "Yes."

"When are you leaving?"

Harley hesitated. "In the morning."

"*What*?" Molly's voice rose.

"I'm only a temporary fill in—"

"Yes, until Maxine comes back, but she's not back for another month." Molly stared at Harley hard. "Did you and

Dad have a fight?"

"No."

"So you are upset about me being bratty."

"*No.*"

"Then why go?"

Harley didn't know how to explain any of this to Molly, not when it was so complicated. "I'm not the best fit for the ranch—"

"That's not true. Daddy's happy with you here. We're happy with you here. Everybody likes having you here. Even JB. He says you're the best thing that's happened to Copper Mountain Ranch, and he's been here almost ten years." Molly approached Harley where she sat on the bed, and put her hands together, in a little prayer. "Don't go," she pleaded. "You have to stay. We need you."

"Oh, Molly—"

"*I* need you," she interrupted. " 'Specially since they're not going to let me go back to school in New York."

Harley reached out to tug on a strand of Molly's warm brown hair. "I'm sure your dad will figure something out."

"But I don't want to go away. I want to be here with Dad. I want to live at home. And I like being here with you here, too. It feels... better." Molly's eyes filled with tears. "You make it better. You make it feel... good. 'Cause you're not like a housekeeper. You're like a... mom. Or at least, like what I think a mom would be."

For a moment Harley couldn't speak. She swallowed

hard, and then again, fighting the awful lump in her throat making it hard to breathe. "Thank you," she said huskily. "That's probably the nicest thing anyone could say to me."

Molly sat down next to Harley on the bed, and looked at her, her small pale brow furrowing. "Don't you want kids, Miss Harley?"

Harley nodded slowly, aching for all that was and all that wasn't and all that could never be.

"But you want your own kids," Molly persisted softly.

Harley bit down into her lip as tears filled her eyes. Her hand shook as she reached up to wipe beneath her eyes, needing to dry the tears before they fell. "I don't know how to answer that."

"Oh, I made you sad!" Molly leaned forward, her eyes searching Harley's. "Don't cry," she crooned, wiping away a tear that had slipped free. "Don't cry. I'm sorry. I always say the wrong thing. Mack says I always talk too much—"

"No, you don't." Harley reached out to cup the girl's cheek. She held Molly's gaze, her own expression fierce. "You're perfect. Absolutely perfect in every way. Don't let anyone tell you otherwise."

Molly nodded and hugged Harley, her small arms squeezing fiercely and Harley hugged the girl back.

"So stay with us," Molly whispered. "I think you're supposed to be with us, Miss Harley."

"And how do you know that?"

"I can't explain it. I just know so."

There were no words.

There was nothing Harley could say. She kissed Molly's forehead and gave the girl a last, fierce hug.

HARLEY COULDN'T SLEEP after Molly left. She was too stirred up, too full of ambivalent emotion.

She didn't want to leave.

She had to leave.

She was already too attached to this family…

It wasn't her family…

As the clock downstairs chimed midnight, Harley gave up on sleep and went down to the kitchen to make tea.

While the water boiled, she added a small log to the burning embers in the fireplace and then remained crouching in front of the fire, letting the red and gold flames warm her.

She felt positively sick about leaving, but that's exactly what worried her. It's why she couldn't let herself stay another day. She'd come here for a job, come here to work, and instead she'd fallen in love with the family.

In nine short days this house, and this family, felt like home.

"I thought I heard you," Brock said, yawning from the shadows of the kitchen doorway.

She rose quickly. "I didn't mean to wake you."

"You didn't. I was thinking about you."

"You look like you were asleep."

He shrugged as he entered the kitchen, dropping into the rocking chair near her. "I guess I was dreaming about you then."

She moved back a couple steps, needing distance. "You shouldn't do that."

"Do what?"

"Dream about me. Think about me. Any of that."

He tipped his head back. "Why not?"

"Because." She sighed, looked away, running a hand across her forehead, aware that it wasn't a very articulate response but her emotions were so raw. She felt so raw even now. Molly's questions had undone her.

"Molly told me she begged you to stay," Brock said quietly.

Harley looked at him sharply.

"She also said she made you cry," he added.

Harley closed her eyes, holding her breath.

"I'm sorry she upset you." Brock's husky voice seemed to burrow deep inside of her. "She means well—"

"I cried because she made me happy," Harley blurted, opening her eyes, tears falling again, already. "She paid me the nicest compliment and I just wish..." Her voice faded and she shook her head. There were no words...no words at all...

"What do you wish?" he asked.

She shook her head. "It doesn't matter. It won't change anything—"

"You never know. Some wishes do come true."

The tea kettle whistled and Brock got to his feet. "I'll make the tea," he said, motioning for Harley to take the rocking chair. "You, sit. Relax. I've got this."

"Why?"

"You've taken care of my ranch hands, my kids, me. Can't I do something for you, just once?"

Harley slowly sat down in the still-warm rocking chair and curled her legs up under her, watching Brock cross the dark kitchen lit by only the firelight. He was so big and powerfully built, the kind of man who looked right in firelight with all those thick muscles and rippling biceps.

She watched him turn off the burner and set out mugs and search for the right tea. It was a pleasure watching him move, so rugged and beautiful in sweat pants and a white T-shirt that hugged him in all the right places.

Looking at him only made her want him more. He'd felt so good last night, pressed up against her. Warm, hard, strong. He'd kissed her with fire, kissed her with need, kissed her as if she were infinitely desirable.

It felt good to be desirable.

It'd made her hope. And wish. Longing for things she didn't have, and might never have again.

A man who loved her deeply.

A man who loved her and would always love her.

A man who wouldn't tire of her even though she'd given him three beautiful children.

A man who would fight to the end to keep his family together…

Her eyes burned and she blinked, clearing her vision to watch Brock walk back across the kitchen, two mugs of tea hooked by the fingers of one hand and a plate of Harley's gingersnap cookies in the other.

"My lady," he said, bowing as he handed her a mug.

She smiled unsteadily as she looked up at him. He looked so lovely in the firelight, his dark hair rumpled and his jaw shadowed, his black lashes lifting, revealing brown, gleaming eyes.

She liked him, a lot.

It was strange and disorienting and bittersweet to feel so much.

Until a few days ago, he hadn't said more than eight words to her at any one time and she had to admit, it had been better when he'd ignored her. She'd been able to maintain her distance when he was detached.

"Thank you, sir," she said, as he set the cookies on the side table next to the rocking chair and retrieved one of the stools from the island and carried it back to the fire, placing it in front of Harley.

He sat down on the stool facing her, and leaned back against the dark wood, long legs extended, looking very relaxed as he sipped his tea.

Harley sipped her tea, too, but felt far from relaxed.

They might look all cozy and domestic sipping herbal tea

in front of the fire, but there was nothing cozy about the tension coiling inside her.

Brock was not soothing company. He didn't calm her down. He wound her up, and ever since he'd entered the kitchen, he'd lit the room up, even though it was still dark.

She didn't know how he did it, either. Wind her up. Turn her on. But last night she literally fell into his arms, and then fell apart for him, and she didn't do that. Harley didn't go through life wanting and desiring. She was far too practical for that.

But Brock was making her want the most impractical things.

Like right now. She was baffled by his energy, a potent male energy that made her aware of things she never thought about, like her body, her lips, her skin.

He was doing it to her again, right now. The tension was incredible. The kitchen was practically crackling and humming.

She was crackling and humming, too, which was baffling, since she hadn't ever hummed for anyone before.

Flushing, she lifted her head, met his gaze. He let her look, too, his dark gaze holding hers, challenging her.

He wanted her.

He wanted to finish what they'd started last night.

Harley's pulse quickened and the silence stretched, wrapping around them, making the spacious kitchen feel very small and private. Intimate.

It wasn't. This was the kitchen, the heart of the house, and even though the kids were asleep, they could come downstairs at any time.

The kids...

She had to remember the twins. Had to remember facts, reality. "Maybe I should go back to bed," she said, shifting uneasily.

"Why?"

"You know why." She licked her upper lip, her mouth suddenly too dry. "Last night."

"What about last night?"

She could feel him across from her, feel him as surely as if he was touching her, just the way he'd touched her last night, his hands beneath her robe, hands cupping, stroking, making her forget everything...

She couldn't afford to forget everything. It was too dangerous. She exhaled in a little rush. "Last night was a mistake."

His dark gaze met hers, held. For a long moment he said nothing, and then his powerful shoulders shrugged. "I've been thinking the same thing."

Her eyes widened. It was the last thing she'd expected him to say. "You were?"

He nodded. "It's good you're going," he added quietly. "It'll be a relief to have you gone."

She stiffened, startled. "Oh."

"Yes, oh," he echoed, setting his mug down. "Because

when you're gone, I won't be tempted to do this." He leaned forward, took her tea from her, placing it on the side table before taking her hand and dragging her to her feet.

"Or this," he said, drawing her toward him, pulling her against him until he had her wedged firmly between his thighs.

"Or this." His hands clasped her face, his thumbs brushing her cheekbones, making her skin tingle and burn. "Such a beautiful woman," he murmured, angling her head to cover her mouth with his.

The kiss was slow and hot and unbearably sexy. His fingers slid into her hair, tangling in the thick weight framing her face as he took his time kissing her, savoring her mouth, exploring the shape of her lips with his lips and tongue.

Last night had been good, but oh, this was better. This kiss was intoxicating, so wickedly good but also so sweet that she felt as if she was melting into a puddle of need, just as if she were dark chocolate or marshmallow crème…

Sighing, she wrapped her arms around Brock's neck, luxuriating in the feel of his warm body, holding him tighter, holding him closer, leaning against him as she no longer trusted her legs to support her. But leaning against him just made her more aware of his desire for her, his erection pressing against her through the soft fabric of his sweatpants.

It would be so easy to touch him, stroke him, and feeling strangely empowered, she slid one hand down his chest, over the bunched bicep in his arm before trailing lower to his side, his hip, his thigh.

She felt him straining against her and it made her even bolder. Curious about him, she caressed the length of him, and there was quite a bit of him to explore.

His breath hitched, and he covered her hand with his, his fingers curving around hers. "I don't know how much more self-control I've got left," he said hoarsely. "This might be a good time to talk about the weather or animal husbandry or crop rotation."

Harley laughed softly. "That's awesome." She laughed again, and leaned back to better see his face. "You know I could discuss all three," she said, trailing her fingers over his cheek and jaw, liking the bristle and bite of his beard beneath her fingertips. "I'm especially well versed in animal husband-ry. That was my minor at Cal Poly."

He turned his face into her hand, kissing her palm. "I forget you're a farm girl."

"I'm good with cows."

"You're the perfect girl."

"Ha!" And yet her heart turned over, aching a little, wishing. Wishing.

Like a child, all those impossible Christmas wishes…

"What would the perfect girl do now, Brock Sheenan?"

"Not go tomorrow."

Oh. She drew a little hiccup of a breath. "But if she did have to go tomorrow, what would she do tonight?"

"Love me all night long."

Oh God.

Overwhelmed by the intensity of emotion rushing through her, rushing through her, Harley leaned forward and kissed Brock, deeply, fiercely, needing him, wanting to feel him and touch him, and yes, love him.

Because she did love him. As impossible and improbable as it was.

But Christmas was the time for miracles. If anything could happen, it could happen now…

"Yes," she murmured against his mouth. "Yes. I want to."

His hand tangled her hair. "You're my perfect girl even if you don't sleep with me, Harley."

"But I want to," she answered, licking her bottom lip, heart thudding. "Where would we go? My room?"

"I don't think your door locks." He hesitated. "But mine does."

"What about the kids?"

"They're asleep."

She stared into his eyes, nervous, excited, and scared, but even more scared of this moment going and never having it again. "We'd have to be *so* quiet."

"Baby, I'm *always* quiet."

She laughed, a real belly aching laugh that made her chest and tummy hurt, and it felt so good to laugh a real laugh, felt so good to be warm and fizzy and excited.

Excited.

And that was the moment she knew. She'd fallen for him, head over heels. There was no playing it safe now. No easy, painless way out.

The log in the fire broke, and the fire crackled and popped, sending a river of sparks into the air.

Harley watched the red hot sparks fly and then disappear.

She felt like one of those sparks now, burning so hot and bright. She wanted her Christmas wish now.

"Let's go," she whispered.

He carried her up the stairs and set her on the bed before silently locking his door. His bed was huge, a big wood four poster, and he stripped off his T-shirt and sweatpants, leaving him naked.

The curtains were open and outside the moon shone high in the sky, reflecting brightly off the thick white drifts of snow, casting a silvery white glow across the bedroom.

She could see Brock, all of him. It was amazing—he was amazing—but this was also intimidating because she had to undress next.

Heart pounding she shrugged off her robe, and then tugged off her pajama top and then finally peeled off the matching bottoms, aware that Brock was just standing, watching.

"What are you thinking?" she whispered, suddenly nervous and painfully shy.

"That you look like an angel on my bed."

Her eyes stung but with the good kind of tears. "You say the nicest things."

"I don't like talking, so I only say what I mean."

She put a hand out, reaching for him. "Come here, before I lose my courage."

"There's no reason to be afraid." He opened the nightstand next to the bed and removed a foil wrapped package from the drawer. "And we can stop at any time. I've waited a long time for you. I can wait another night or two."

Brock stretched out on the bed next to her, covering them with the folded blanket from the foot of the bed.

"Kiss me," she whispered, drawing his head down to hers.

"Absolutely," he answered, rolling her onto her back and settling between her thighs.

THE SEX WAS so good. The sex was *unbelievably* good.

"Wow," she murmured, cheek resting on his chest, her pulse still racing, her body warm and languid. "You do that like a rock star."

He laughed and stroked her hair. "You've been with a lot of rock stars?"

She smiled, enjoying the husky vibration of his laughter and the steady thud of his heart beneath her cheek. She liked it when he laughed, and loved it when he teased her.

And now this intense physical connection...

If she wasn't careful she'd get completely swept away by

the intensity and passion, but she had to remember that the sex—although very good and very hot—wasn't love. It was just pleasure. Physical gratification. And the physical couldn't replace love, friendship, respect.

All she had to do was remember David to know why a relationship couldn't be based on chemistry and passion. Chemistry and passion would fade, and then what?

Harley didn't want to fall in love just for the thrill of it. She wanted what she'd thought she'd had when she married David. A family. A future.

Brock's hand slipped from her hair, to trace down her spine, his calloused palm so warm against her bare skin. "You're thinking," he said.

"I am," she agreed, regrets creeping in.

"Tell me."

She drew a deep breath, hating how quickly her emotions were changing, hating how all the good feelings were fading, leaving her scared, sad.

It was hard to feel so much, and want so much.

It was hard to care so much when she was leaving in the morning.

"Come on," he insisted, shifting her onto her back, and rising on his elbow to look down at her. "Talk to me."

"I don't want tomorrow to be weird," she said roughly.

He lifted a strand of hair from her cheek, smoothing it from her face. "Why would it be weird?"

"You know. Saying goodbye. And then leaving the kids."

Her throat ached. "It's going to be hard to leave... them."

The corner of his mouth lifted. Deep grooves bracketed his lips. "Just them?" he teased, dipping his head to kiss her brow, her nose, her lips.

A tingle shot through her and her tummy flipped at the trio of tender kisses. "And you." She struggled to smile. "I kind of like you, tough guy."

"So stay," he said, kissing her cheek, her jaw, her chin. "Why go? Where do you have to go?"

His kisses were making her pulse race, and his words were making her want things but her head balked. Her head was practical and real. She was practical and real. She'd been swept away by passion once before and she couldn't afford to get carried away again. "It sounds like a horribly depressing romance novel. *The Housekeeper & The Cowboy*."

"Perhaps it'd sound better if you called it, *The House-keeper's Cowboy*."

"That's even worse."

He kissed the corner of her mouth, and then just beneath her lower lip, making it quiver. "Maybe we just need some adjectives, fancy it up."

"You have suggestions?" she asked.

He kissed the other corner of her mouth, lightly, so lightly that her breath caught in her throat. "How about... *The Hot Housekeeper's Lonely Cowboy*."

"Too pathetic," she whispered, toes curling with pleasure. The man could *kiss*.

He nuzzled below her ear, and then kissed his way down her neck. "Your turn," he said. "Make it good. Make me want to buy that story."

She giggled then sighed, as his mouth traced her collarbone making her shiver and need. She pressed her knees together, closed her eyes, her body tingling everywhere. "*The Hot Housekeeper's Sexy Cowboy.*"

"Now there's a story I want to read," he murmured, moving over her, his big body shifting between her thighs, his erection pressing against her inner thigh. He kissed down, his lips capturing one pebbled nipple. He sucked and she arched up, her hips rocking against his.

Brock's fingers twined with hers. He slid her hands up the mattress, over her head, trapping her.

She liked it. Liked the tension in her arms, the tension in their bodies, it felt hot and raw.

It'd be so easy to open to him. To just take him. She wanted to take him, loved the weight of him, and the feel of him. Loved the way they felt together. But couldn't make love again without protection. "Have another condom?" she whispered.

"More where that one came from… in the bunk house."

"We don't need *The Sexy Cowboy's Pregnant Housekeeper.*"

"Not unless she wanted to be *The Sexy Cowboy's Hot Wife,*" he answered, shifting so that the tip of his shaft stroked her, making nerves dance.

"Ha."

"We'd make a beautiful baby."

She no longer felt like laughing. Her eyes burned. It hurt to swallow. "That's not funny."

He released her hands, cupped her face, kissing her slowly. "It wasn't meant to be funny." His dark head lifted, he gazed down at her, dark eyes somber, expression grave. "I never thought I'd ever marry again. But I can see you here, with us. You fit with us. I think I'd like being married to you."

She didn't even know how to respond to that. She couldn't wrap her head around any of it. Stay here. Marry him. Be a surrogate mom to his kids.

She'd have a family. It'd be his family.

And that was the problem.

It'd be *his* family. She'd be the surrogate. The fill-in. He could replace her, too. She couldn't bear being replaced, not again.

"It's too soon," she said. "Too fast. You don't even know me. A month from now you might feel differently—"

"I won't."

"You don't know that."

"I do. I'm not reckless. I don't make promises and break them. If I make a promise, I keep it. And if I promise to love you and cherish you all the days of my life, I will."

Just like he still loved Amy…

And perhaps that should have scared her, that he still

loved Amy, but it didn't. It reassured her. He had loved his wife. He had been faithful to her memory all these years. His steadfast love gave Harley hope that Brock could be faithful to her.

She closed her eyes, held her breath. It'd be so easy to capitulate. To just give in to the miracle of it all.

Christmas wishes, Christmas dreams…

But what would happen after the holidays were over and it was a new year? How would this work…?

Maxine.

The ranch.

The twins.

The twins.

She exhaled in a small painful puff of air. "Mack and Molly."

"Yes?"

"They've never had to share you with anyone before. They could grow to resent me."

"They won't."

"They could."

He kissed her again. "Then we deal with it."

"You make it all sound too easy."

"Because I think it is easy, after everything we've both been through."

She reached up to touch his cheek. His skin was so warm and his beard rasped her fingertips. Lightly she scraped her nails across his rough jaw. "My family will say I've lost my mind."

"And mine will say the same thing, until they meet you, and then they'll know what I know."

"And what is that?"

"That you being here wasn't an accident. You were meant to be here. You were sent to be here."

Her chest burned, hot and tender. "Who knew you were so good with words?"

"Not selling you. I'm telling you what I know, what I believe. God brought you here to Marietta for a reason. He knew we needed you, and He knew you needed us, and He put his angels to work and produced a Christmas miracle."

"Stop," she whispered, tears filling her eyes.

"Never. Not if it means letting you go. Can't lose you, Harley. I've waited too long for you. Have prayed too long for you." The corner of his mouth lifted, but there were shadows in his dark eyes, and a hint of his old grief. "Don't break my heart now, baby. Not when I have hope again."

Hope.

Hope.

The hot tears blinded her, falling fast, too fast. She'd lived so long without hope. She'd looked so long with pain. "I can't fall in love with you all and then be sent away."

He dipped his head, kissing her cheeks where they were wet. "Won't ever send you away. We are yours. You are home."

Chapter Eight

S HE COULDN'T SAY yes.

She didn't say yes.

It had all sounded so perfect, but that's what scared her. It was too perfect to be true.

The great sex, the laughter, the beautiful words in Brock's cozy moonlit bedroom.

It was a Christmas Hallmark movie and God knows, she didn't watch those. They were so sweet and hopeful they just made her sad.

So she told him no, telling him as kindly as she could, that as wonderful as his offer sounded, she couldn't accept. It was all happening too fast. But if it was meant to be, they'd find each other later, and try again when the timing was better.

He'd listened in silence. "Better timing? What does that mean?"

"It means…" her voice faded. Her stomach hurt, so full of short sharp pains that it felt as if she'd been eating barbed wire. "It means… I've known you not quite two weeks, and your kids just six days, and we can't risk hurting them, or each other, by being impulsive, no matter how romantic it seems."

He'd said nothing for a long time and then he rolled away and sat up on the edge of the bed, his big muscular back to her, his powerful legs on the floor. "Yeah, Mr. Romantic, that's me." And then he'd rose and walked to his bathroom, closed the door and took a long shower.

Harley had returned to her bed on the third floor, her room frigid, her sheets icy cold.

She'd cried into her pillow.

Cried because she'd hurt him and cried because she'd hurt herself. It was brutal telling him no, brutal telling her heart no. But she had to keep focused on facts and the big picture.

They hadn't known each other long.

He had two children who were so vulnerable right now. His children didn't need drama. They'd been through so much. They should be protected. Surrounded by stability, security.

She was doing the right thing, saying no. Her head was sure of it.

But that didn't stop her from crying.

IN THE MORNING she was up at five. It was dark outside. It'd be dark for at least another hour and a half.

She took a quick shower and then dressed, tucking her pajamas and vanity bag into her suitcase. She was totally packed now. When the new housekeeper arrived, Harley would just grab her suitcase and go.

They'd keep the goodbyes brief. No big emotional scene. Nothing drawn out. She was Dutch. She could do this. Quick, crisp, clean.

That's the way goodbyes were meant to be.

Her kids came to mind, their bright eyes and big smiles as they'd left her that last morning, smiling, waving, saying they loved her. Saying they'd see her soon.

Talk about a quick goodbye. They'd walked out the door and she'd never seen them again.

Life was brutal that way. Life was capricious and hard and harsh. Harley couldn't rush into hard and harsh, she couldn't go there again…

Or could she?

She thought of Mack and Molly and how they'd spent their entire life wondering what it'd be like to have a mom. They were just babies themselves and still in need of so much love and TLC.

Could she face her fear for them?

Could she face her fear to love their dad?

Harley wished, hoped, but didn't know. And yet she had to know. She had to believe.

But the confidence wasn't there inside of her. She wasn't sure of anything right now, too caught up in the emotions sweeping through her.

Hope, wish, dream, need.

Heartbreak, loss, pain, grief.

Which was bigger, which was stronger?

Love was stronger, but was there enough love here? Was there enough love to mend their hearts and make them work?

How would she know? How could she know?

Leaving her suitcase by her bedroom door, she turned off her bedroom light and headed downstairs.

IN THE KITCHEN, the fire was already crackling and burning.

Dark, rich coffee brewed on the counter.

Brock was up.

And knowing that made her want him, but she couldn't waffle and send mixed signals.

Taking her time, taking things slow was right. Being careful and thoughtful was best.

And yet... and yet... part of her yearned to just run to him. Run and say, *forgive me. Keep me. Love me.*

He would, too. She knew it. Knew that he might not be a perfect man but he was honest and tough and strong and real.

She'd watched him here on this ranch, and he did nothing halfway. When he was worried one of the young calves was missing, he'd gone back out in the dark, in a snowstorm, to track it down. And he hadn't come home until he'd found him.

A man of his word.

A man of the word. He'd waited for her. Prayed for her.

She poured herself a cup of coffee and went to the window above the sink to look out. Stars still shone brightly overhead. She searched the dark sky for a sign... her own North Star.

And then something amazing happened.

The sky lit up in a thousand colored lights. Red, blue, green, yellow, gold, white. Light after light glowing brightly, revealing the white landscape glittering in a fresh clean layer of newly fallen slow.

Leaning toward the window, she realized that it wasn't the sky filled with lights but the big tree in the corner of the yard.

The huge pine tree—twenty-something feet tall—was covered in brilliant glowing colorful light.

The huge pine tree was a Christmas tree.

Oh, God.

The biggest most beautiful Christmas tree she'd ever seen. Here. Here. And she knew who'd done it and she knew why he'd done it and she didn't think she could bear it.

It would have taken hours.

It would have taken all night.

She put her head down on the counter, and cried.

Crying because it was too much. It was. There weren't words for things like this. Weren't words for things so beautiful and magical. Life-changing. Momentous. Life-changing. Healing. Life changing.

Hope.

Faith.

Grace.

God.

And Harley just cried.

How could she leave them? How could she go? How could she leave when there was nowhere else she'd rather be?

"We think you're supposed to be here," Molly said, her voice soft and hushed on the far side of the kitchen.

Harley straightened, turning abruptly, wiping her cheeks dry. It was impossible. The tears kept falling.

Molly and Mack were in their pajamas and yet beneath their pajamas were snow boots and snowflakes glittered on their hair and dusted their pink cheeks.

"We know you're supposed to be here," Mack corrected. "It's the plan."

"The plan?" Harley whispered.

Molly walked to Harley and took her hand. "We figured it out last night after Dad told us about your kids, how you lost your kids, like we lost our mom."

Mack nodded. "We couldn't sleep 'cause we knew why you were here. Mom sent you here. She knew you missed your kids and she knew we missed her…" His voice faded.

For a moment there was only silence.

Molly squeezed Harley's hand. "We think our mom is in

heaven taking care of your kids," Molly said quietly. "Because I bet even in heaven, kids need a mom, and I bet my mom would be a good one. Dad said she was a good mom. Dad said she loved us."

"I'm sure she was the best mom ever," Harley whispered, the lump so big in her throat that she was afraid she'd cry all over again.

"We bet you were a really good mom, too," Molly added. "A really, really good mom. Because you're not even our mom and you're really, really nice to us."

Harley held her breath, praying for control. But when tears fell, Molly's cool fingers were there, on Harley's cheeks, carefully wiping them away.

"We like you," Molly whispered in a low voice. "We like you a lot, Harley, so please don't go."

Mack nodded. "I think, we think, we *know*, Mom sent you to us. That's why Dad put the lights on Mom's tree."

"Come on," Molly said, tugging on her hand. "Let's go outside. Let's go see Mom's tree."

"Why do you call it Mom's tree?" Harley asked, as they pulled her though the hall, past the stairs, and out the front door where the massive cedar tree lit with endless strands of colored light.

"Because Mom planted the tree for Dad," Mack said, drawing Harley down the front steps, into the thick powdered snow. "It was her wedding present to him. She planted it near the house so he'd always remember how much she loved him."

They moved around the side of the enormous glowing tree and there was Brock, waiting for her.

"Amy said the tree would always be here, protecting me, and the house, and our family with love," Brock said, moving toward her, taking her hands in his. "And she has. She's done her part. But she knows we need more. We need you."

Brock dug out of his pocket a ring case, and snapped it open, revealing a sparkling diamond ring. An engagement ring. "I'm not giving up, Harley. Won't give up. I'm a fighter, and I'm fighting for you, and I'll fight for you as long as I have to."

Harley stared at Brock and then at the ring, understanding, but not understanding. "When did you buy the ring?"

"Yesterday with the kids in Marietta."

The twins nodded. "We helped pick it out," Mack said, shyly. "We wanted you to have a really big diamond, too."

"Girls like big diamonds," Molly said.

"You're serious?" Harley whispered, looking at Brock. "You mean this?"

"Oh, I absolutely mean this, Harley. I've been up all night trying to show you somehow that we need you here, that we want you here. Just have faith. We do."

Have faith.

But she did. It's all that had gotten her through. And now she was here, and was it her faith that had brought her here?

"I do, too," she answered huskily.

"Good." He leaned forward kissed her. And then he got down on one knee in the snow and took her hand, holding it firmly in his. "Harley Diekerhoff, will you marry me?"

"Yes," she whispered.

"Yes?" he asked, making sure.

For a moment there was just silence. It was a perfect silence, accompanied by a sense of peace. A perfect peace.

"Yes," she answered, as he rose and swept her up in his arms. "Yes," she repeated, laughing through happy tears. "Yes, yes, yes."

"I love you," he whispered against her mouth, kissing her.

"I love you, too."

He kept kissing her and the twins cheered. And then there was even more cheering, loud raucous cheering and whistling and Harley realized that all the boys from the bunk house were here, too, watching.

But it was good.

All was right in the world.

Faith had brought her here.

Miracles were possible.

And love would keep them together.

THE END

From *New York Times* Bestselling author
Jane Porter comes…

THE TAMING OF THE SHEENANS SERIES

If you enjoyed *Christmas at Copper Mountain*, you will love
the rest of the Sheenan brothers!

Christmas At Copper Mountain
Book 1: Brock Sheenan's story

The Tycoon's Kiss
Book 2: Troy Sheenan's story

The Kidnapped Christmas Bride
Book 3: Trey Sheenan's story

The Taming of the Bachelor
Book 4: Dillion Sheenan's story

A Christmas Miracle for Daisy
Book 5: Cormac Sheenan's story

The Lost Sheenan's Bride
Book 6: Shane Sheenan's story

Available now at your favorite online retailer!

About the Author

New York Times and USA Today bestselling author of fifty romance and women's fiction titles, **Jane Porter** has been a finalist for the prestigious RITA award five times and won in 2014 for Best Novella with her story, *Take Me, Cowboy*, from Tule Publishing. Today, Jane has over 12 million copies in print, including her wildly successful, *Flirting With Forty*, picked by Redbook as its Red Hot Summer Read, and reprinted six times in seven weeks before being made into a Lifetime movie starring Heather Locklear. A mother of three sons, Jane holds an MA in Writing from the University of San Francisco and makes her home in sunny San Clemente, CA with her surfer husband, Ty Gurney, his vintage cars and trucks, and their two dogs.

Visit Jane at JanePorter.com.

Thank you for reading

CHRISTMAS AT COPPER MOUNTAIN

If you enjoyed this book, you can find more from all our great authors at TulePublishing.com, or from your favorite online retailer.

TULE
PUBLISHING

Made in the USA
Charleston, SC
28 July 2016